WHO ~~I AM~~

I'M NOT

For Cathy & Phil,

who know exactly
who they are.

Thanks so much
for everything,

'17

WHO ~~I AM~~ I'M NOT

TED STAUNTON

ORCA BOOK PUBLISHERS

Library and Archives Canada Cataloguing in Publication

Staunton, Ted, 1956-
Who I'm not / Ted Staunton.

Issued also in electronic formats.
ISBN 978-1-4598-0434-0

I. Title.
PS8587.T334W56 2013   jc813'.54   C2013-901870-0

First published in the United States, 2013
Library of Congress Control Number: 2013935300

Summary: A kid in trouble with the law assumes the identity of a boy
who vanished three years before.

MIX
Paper from
responsible sources
FSC
www.fsc.org   FSC® C004071

ANCIENT FOREST ™
FRIENDLY

*Orca Book Publishers is dedicated to preserving the environment and
has printed this book on Forest Stewardship Council® certified paper.*

Orca Book Publishers gratefully acknowledges the support for its publishing
programs provided by the following agencies: the Government of Canada through
the Canada Book Fund and the Canada Council for the Arts, and the Province of British
Columbia through the BC Arts Council and the Book Publishing Tax Credit.

Design by Teresa Bubela
Cover image by Andrew Wooldridge and Teresa Bubela

ORCA BOOK PUBLISHERS   ORCA BOOK PUBLISHERS
PO Box 5626, Stn. B   PO Box 468
Victoria, BC Canada   Custer, WA USA
V8R 6S4   98240-0468

www.orcabook.com
Printed and bound in Canada.

16 15 14 13 • 4 3 2 1

For Will and Margaret,
who both know who they are

Men...have an extraordinary knack of lending themselves to deception, a sort of curious and inexplicable propensity to allow themselves to be led by the nose with their eyes open.

—Joseph Conrad, *The Mirror of the Sea*

ONE

It's easier to tell you who I'm not. I'm not Kerry Ludwig or Sean Callahan. I'm not David Alvierez or Peter McLeod or Frank Rolfe. I've kind of wished I was David Alvierez. I don't look Latino or anything, but it sounds exotic. Anyway, I've been all those guys, but none of them was me.

And I'm not Danny Dellomondo either, no matter what I said. If I were Danny, I wouldn't be telling you this, would I? I mean, I couldn't. The only reason I became him was because Harley died.

We were working this high-end mall in Tucson. Harley was doing switch-backs on debit card pin machines, two in fancy clothing stores and one—he said it was the jackpot—in this executive-type fitness club. I was decoying. He'd lifted the store's machines the month before.

Harley had switched them for ones he'd gotten from this guy Dennis. The plan was, Dennis's machines would store up a whole month's worth of pin numbers and info. Then, when we switched them back, Dennis could download it all and tap into all these rich people's bank accounts.

"They'll still notice, even if they're rich," I said.

"Naw," Harley told me, "that's the beauty part. With so many numbers, you just do a little bit, over and over, from each one, so they *don't* notice. And if someone does, who cares? You've still got all the rest. It adds up to major coin."

We weren't getting cut into the *major* coin—we were hired hands. Dennis was paying straight cash for the switches. We moved around a lot, so even if they ever did look at the security videos, nobody would recognize us. Harley said we were going to Seattle as soon as Dennis paid up.

The clothing stores were routine. The back-to-school sales were on, but it was the slackest part of the afternoon. We were pretty duded up to fit in—Harley was always really careful about clothes. I'd go in first and get the clerks away from the desk to help me pick something for my mom's birthday. Then I'd say I'd forgotten what her size was and promise to come back.

I liked decoying. People got right into it, probably because most of them think teenagers are supposed to be all attitude. If they really got into it, I'd take a while. I didn't have to—Harley only needed a few seconds to unplug this and plug in that (you should have seen him deal cards)—but it was nice; I could tell I was making their day. I'd make up all kinds of stuff, until I'd half-believe it myself. Feeling good is what we sell, Harley liked to say when we were scamming. If a store lady was *really* nice to me and was about the right age, I'd tell her she should be my mother. That would always make her laugh and get blushy, so you could tell she liked it. Once in a while I'd find myself wondering if she *was* my mother, maybe even wishing it a little bit, you know. Which is strange, because I've imagined lots of parents, but I never saw them working in a store.

After we hit the stores, we met in the food court and then did the health club. Harley said he was my dad and got me sent on a tour to see if I liked it enough for him to take out a family membership. This studly guy with too much tan walked me to the elliptical trainers and all the weight machines. I bet the ladies liked him, but he creeped me out. He was completely hairless. Every so often he'd check himself out in the mirror. I glanced back at Harley; he already had the switch done. I told the guy I'd think about it. He gave me his business card.

Outside, I remember, Harley stopped to put on his two-tone shades and settle the collar of his yellow polo shirt out over his blazer. Then he adjusted the cuffs of the blazer too, so his big silver watch showed. Harley was just so about everything, especially his hair. He was getting thin on top, and he was short enough that you'd notice.

He was carrying an empty laptop case and a small gym bag that he'd stashed the pin machines in. He looked like Joe Business, just done a workout.

He took out a pack of gum and popped in a couple of pieces, and we started across the parking lot for the van. Everything was bright and glary, and the heat was pounding up from the pavement in shock waves. August in Tucson is no joke. I was dragging, but it didn't matter to Harley. Harley never walked—he strutted.

"Good day's work," Harley said around his chewing.

"How much will Dennis pay?" I asked.

"I'll handle that." Harley didn't look at me while we talked. I knew he was scoping out the parking lot for incidental action. *You ever had too much money?* he liked to ask me, even though it wasn't a real question. I never had any money unless he gave me some, and I had no clue how much we—I mean, he—had.

"Hey, hey," Harley said. "Check it out. You see him? Fat Boy."

I knew by now what to look for. Sure enough, two rows of cars over a lumpy guy with spiky hair was huffing and puffing, a big bag from the mall's stereo store in each hand and a laptop case slung over his shoulder.

"Go," Harley said, chewing faster. "Good car, we do it."

It was the key game—easy and just exciting enough to be fun. I peeled away and hustled through the heat and the parked cars to the row just past Fat Boy. Then I slowed down, staying behind him. He stopped at a black Lexus. Perfect. I ducked down. I heard his door locks click open. I saw him slinging the stuff into the back seat. He was sweating in the sunshine; you could see the dark patch where his shirt stuck to his back. He opened the driver's door, and as he got in, I crept to the car right behind his. Harley was strolling in front of the Lexus, pretending to look at his big watch from behind his shades. Fat Boy reached for his shoulder belt. I stood up and stepped forward. Harley looked up from his watch. "Hey!" he yelled to Fat Boy. "Hey!" He rapped on the car's hood, then pointed. "He's keying your car!"

Fat Boy freaked. He was scrambling around so much, the Lexus started rocking. Then he tumbled out all red-faced and wild-eyed, yelling, "Hey! You little—"

I froze at the back on the passenger side, as if I was scared stiff. Really, I was counting to three. He came at me. I ran.

It was no problem to outrun him; I'm small for my age. All I had to do was distract him long enough for Harley to scoop everything and get away. Then I'd loop back to the van and we'd be gone.

I could hear Fat Boy gasping behind me, the slap of his loafers on the pavement. We were far enough away by now. *Never look back*, Harley always said, but I did it this once, as I sped up. Fat Boy's face was purple. He stumbled, and his hand came up. There was something in it. It could have been a Blackberry. It could have been a gun. *That* scared me. I yelled as I dodged around a monster SUV. Two rows of cars over, I glimpsed Harley's head. It snapped around at the sound of my voice. Then I heard three things all in a row: a horn blare, brakes shriek and this muffled *clunk*, like something falling over in a closet. Then Harley was dead.

TWO

I guess I could've got away right then. What I would have got away *to*, I couldn't tell you. I had five bucks in my pocket and the Frank Rolfe ID. Harley had everything else, even the key to the motel room, which was way across town anyway.

So maybe it didn't matter that I ran back to Harley. I was still there, stunned, numb, kneeling on the pavement beside him and the blackening puddle spreading under his head, when the ambulance and the cops showed up and the little crowd that had gathered moved aside. One of the ambulance people put an oxygen mask on Fat Boy, who was still gasping, slumped against a light pole.

I don't know how long it was before I was sitting on a plastic lawn chair in an office, and this guy who said his name was Josh was talking to me. By then, I was wide awake and more. I could've felt a mosquito flying in the next room. I'd met lots of Joshes before, back in the Bad Time, and usually in offices like this. Only difference was, my feet didn't always reach the ground then.

"Frank," he said, "you understand I'm not police? You're at Youth Services—it's a shelter. My job is to protect you. You've had a crazy time today. All I'm here to do is help." He gave me a business card. It was my day for cards.

I stuffed it in my pocket and nodded. Harley was dead, but I wasn't feeling that, only how the room was throbbing with Bad Time vibes. I was fighting down the panic, panting. Whenever Harley had been really pissed with me, especially when I was younger, all he'd had to say was *You want to go back to the Bad Time?* and I'd cave, instantly. No matter what, I *never* wanted to go back to the Bad Time. My memories of it had gotten all hazy and jumbled, but that just made it scarier, like something changing shape in the shadows. All I wanted was to get out of here, even if all I had was five bucks and bad ID.

Josh slung one leg up onto the mess on his desk. His shoes were black Converse high tops. His short-sleeved shirt was all rumply. *Trust me* cool. He leaned back in his chair, but he kept his eyes locked on me. They were dark. Behind him, his computer screen still glowed; he'd been typing when they brought me in. Above his shoulder, I could just make out *CASE MANAGEMENT STRATEGIES*. I knew all about case-management strategies—the story of my life. Somewhere, a file about me was full of them. He said, "Is there anybody you want to call, or want me to call?"

I shook my head. "No, it's okay. I should just go." My voice wobbled.

Josh pressed his lips together. "Well, Frank, the question is, where to? According to your ID, you're fifteen, which makes you a minor. And from Michigan. Have you got family here in Tucson? Friends?"

"Oh sure," I said. "There's the Ludwigs, and the McLeods, the Lombards. And the Alvierezes, they live really close. You don't have to call or anything. I can just walk."

I stood up fast. It made me dizzy.

"Frank," Josh said gently, "chill."

I sat back down, shoving my hands in my pockets so he wouldn't see them tremble. I was wearing Gap cargo shorts to go with the preppy-rich-kid look. They made my legs look skinny, which probably made me seem even smaller and younger than I was. I didn't know if that was good or bad.

Josh said, "The cops told me about the IDs in the van, with a lot of other stuff. A bag full of pin machines, et cetera. You want to tell me anything else?"

"I told *them*. I didn't even *know* that guy. I was just passing, like everybody else."

Josh nodded. He took his leg off his desk and put his elbows on it instead. Then he cupped his face in his hands and looked at me some more. He scratched under his chin;

he was one of those guys with the three-day-beard look. I'd probably like that look if I could do it. Then he said, "The cops said you were running the key game."

I wrinkled up my face. "What's the key game?"

Josh just shrugged, his chin still in his hands. "Something the cops think you were doing. Not my problem. I hope not yours, but they're probably going to want to talk to you about it. Me, I'm not asking. My job is to get you somewhere safe. To do that, I have to know who you are. So, who are you, Frank?"

And there it was. The Question. I looked straight back at him. "I dunno," I said. It was true, but that didn't matter. They never believe you when you tell the truth.

Sure enough, Josh let that hang, still watching me. After a minute, he said, "Okay. Listen, you're weirded out. Who wouldn't be? Why don't you take a little time?" He stood up. He was tall and skinny. His rumply shirt was hanging out, too short. "I'm gonna get a coffee. You want anything to eat or drink?"

I shook my head. My heart was pounding in my ears.

"Cool," he said. "Change your mind, I'll be out front. Take a break; chill for a while. You want to use the phone or anything, go ahead. Remember, I'm supposed to help, not hassle. If there's some place you need to get back to, some way I can help you go forward..." He shrugged, cocked his head and gave me a half smile. Then he walked out and closed the door.

I hunched in the chair. Harley was dead. The Bad Time was all around me. For a minute I couldn't move at all. Joshes didn't move you forward, they sent you around in circles. I wasn't going back. I was going to get out of here, no matter what. I stood up. The office opened into the front room, so I couldn't walk out. No outside windows either.

What would Harley do? I pulled my hands out of my pockets. My armpits went cold in the air-conditioning. There were sweat circles under the arms of my Tommy shirt. I took a deep breath and unclenched my fists. Something was crumpled in my hand: Josh's card and the one from the guy at the health club.

I tossed them on the mess on the desk. Everybody had a name. I'd had lots of them. I needed another, one that would at least buy me some time and maybe some distance, far enough away from here to figure out what I should do next. A name to save me from the Bad Time.

What would Harley do? There was a bulletin board with a No Smoking sticker and posters of missing kids pinned up; a map of North America was stuck to the wall above the shelves. Papers, binders, dirty mugs…Josh was a slob. Even his computer monitor was messed up with those little yellow sticky notes. The screen had gone dark. I went around the desk to the computer and jiggled the mouse. The screen brightened. *CASE MANAGEMENT STRATEGIES.* Josh had forgotten to log out.

It was my first break all day. I sat down and took another deep breath. I minimized the screen and opened a new browser window. All I needed now was something to search for. What? A name? Who? What would get me out of here? I swiveled in Josh's chair. Binders, the map, a bulletin board with pictures of runaway kids. I swiveled back to the computer. *Report due Tuesday*, said one sticky note. *Ellen B'day*, said another. Some phone numbers, then a bunch of stickies all down one side of the monitor. *Houston/G, A/Grand Rapids Mi?De./Pomona Ca* and, at the bottom, *Ch Connect KC Mo*. My knees started bouncing. All at once I knew what Harley would do.

I typed *Missing Children* and looked again at the map, far from Arizona. Ontario was the first place I saw, up north in Canada. I remembered Ontario, California. One time a couple years back, Harley and I had made a big score there with an accident-insurance scam. I'd had to wear one of those white padded collar things for a week, but Harley had said it was more than worth it. Maybe Ontario, Canada, would be lucky too. I typed it in and hit the Enter key.

In the front room, voices rose and fell. The whole time I was online, I was scared someone would come in to check on me. No one did, though, and after about half an hour I had three possibles. In the end I picked the kid who had been gone the longest time, three years. He'd been twelve then. Where was I when I was twelve? I didn't want to remember. I memorized this kid instead.

I'm good at memorizing—Harley made sure I was. He used to make me play memory games as we drove.

Then I checked out where the kid was from on Earth Eye and memorized that too. I didn't know if they had funny accents or talked a different language up in Canada. It didn't matter. All I needed to do was get everyone confused long enough for me to get away. I clicked back through the screens, closing them as I went, cleared the history and got out from behind the desk. While I waited for the monitor to go dark, I stuck the business cards back in my pocket. Names can come in handy.

The monitor blanked. Harley was gone. I was on my own. I walked out into the front room. Josh was slouched in a chair, holding a Starbucks tall cup, laughing about something with two hardcore-looking girls. He turned and saw me.

I waited a heartbeat. I said, "My name is Danny."

"Hey, later," Josh said to the girls. He stood up, tossing the cup at the wastebasket. Then he walked toward me.

THREE

My name is Danny Dellomondo. I was born November 9, 1994. I am short and slim, with curly black hair, a long nose and a cocky, wise-guy kind of smile. My eyes used to be gray-green. I had a mole on my right shoulder blade, a scar on my right calf where I got cut by a wire fence when I was little. I'm right-handed. I like honey-garlic wings, cookie dough ice cream, Medal of Honor on PlayStation, metal bands, Star Wars and mirrored aviator sunglasses. I toe out when I walk. I use the word sucker a lot. My mother is Carleen. My older half brother is Tyson and my older half sister is Shannon. I live at 1787 Coach House Road, Grafton, Ontario, K2R 3P5.

I disappeared the afternoon of Tuesday, April 27, 2006, when I didn't take the school bus home and hung out with friends instead. About 5:30 I phoned Tyson on a friend's cell *and asked for a ride. Carleen was supposed to take me to the mall that night and I was scared she'd be mad and change her mind if I was late. Tyson said no. I started walking. I was wearing a black rapper's toque with a little brim turned to one side, a blue puffy vest, a black Slayer jersey, baggy jeans slung low over Simpsons boxers, and gray Vans skate shoes. I was carrying a purple and black backpack with* Led Zeppelin *written on one side in marker. I had a gold chain with a letter* D *on it around my neck. At the corner of Dairy Street and County Road Two, my friends went one way and I went the other. That was the last time anyone saw me.*

Until yesterday in Tucson, Arizona.

I stood in the washroom, staring into the mirror, running over the sketchy line I'd fed Josh about being kidnapped and held captive.

My biggest problem when I'm snowing a mark is that I get carried away. I say too much. I'm probably saying too much right now. Anyway, this time I'd done my best to keep it simple, even if it sounded stupid. I'd tried to follow Harley's rules: *No details, no confusion* and *It's not what you say, it's how you say it.* So I made it too awful for me to talk about—I stopped and started and shrugged and looked away, like I'd done all those times in all those principals' offices back in the Bad Time.

I only got fancy once, because parts of Danny's description didn't match me. That came after I said I'd woken up in a place with barred windows where everyone spoke a different language. I whispered, "I…just…they…

they did something to my eyes. With a needle. It hurt. Now they're brown." I twisted my leg around. "And I had this mark on my leg where I cut it when I was little. They took it off too." Could you do that stuff? I didn't know. I think it was all in a spy story I'd read in some crummy motel where they didn't have cable. Did it matter? *It's not what you say, it's how you say it.*

"Why did they do that?" Josh had asked, still leaning back, watching.

I'd hugged my elbows, as if I was cold. "They said that way…no one would believe…and they wanted…me to… us to…look…uh…certain ways…for…"

Josh's Conversed foot came down off the desk. "There were more kids?"

"Yeah."

"How many?"

I hugged myself harder and rocked back and forth. "I don't know. They changed."

He gave a low half whistle–half whisper. Then he said, "I know it's hard to trust anyone, but the main thing you have to remember is that you're safe here."

I'd kept my head down. I heard him swing his chair to his darkened computer monitor. "I understand how tough this is for you. Let me do some checking."

Bingo.

I'd figured it would take Josh a couple of days to check things out. That would have given me time to figure out how to steal some coin and duck out of there before it all came apart. It didn't happen that way. About three hours later, I was staring at a piece of pizza while the suppertime news blared on a TV outside Josh's office. I was listening for something about Harley when Josh came in and said, "We've reached your family, Danny. They're on the phone. You think you can talk to them?"

I'd freaked, but I couldn't show it. Part of me knew I should say no and stall for time, but part of me said I had to go for it, that this was a test, almost. Maybe it was the way Josh was so fake relaxed about it. His voice and his slouch said *it's cool*, but his eyes were locked on mine again, and they seemed extra dark. I nodded. He picked up a cordless phone from its cradle on the desk and punched a button on it. "Yes, ma'am," he said into it. "I have him here with me now, and he's willing to speak with you. Hold on, please."

He'd held the phone out to me, then raised his eyebrows and mouthed, *Your sister, okay?* I nodded again and lifted the phone to my ear, making sure to wrap my hand around the mouthpiece to muffle my voice, the way I'd seen Harley do it a million times. "Hello?"

A woman's voice quavered, "Danny?"

At least they spoke English in Canada. What else could I do? I mumbled, "Yeah. Is that Shan—" Right there, I'd lost it. It was too crazy. My mouth had gone dry and the rest of her name disappeared. I felt Josh's eyes boring into me. I figured I'd blown it.

There was a gasp on the other end of the line. Then the voice said, "It's Shan, Danny, it's Shan." Then I heard muffled voices, urgent-sounding, almost like an argument.

Another voice had come on then, this one razor-sharp. "Who is this?"

I'd wrapped my hand tighter around the receiver and turned away from Josh. I went with it; I had no choice. "It's Danny. I—I want to come home." Why not? In a way it was even true.

Silence. Could I hear her breathing? Then there was the crumply sound of a hand over the phone and more voices, almost yelling. What were they saying? I was sweating again. Then the Shannon voice was back, shaking. "You just stay safe where you are. I'm coming to get you."

And less than a day later, she was here. Or almost here. I hadn't even had a chance to run, let alone score some cash. For all that *I'm here to help* crap, old Josh had made sure to stick me in a "secure residential facility" overnight, where I'd "lost" my five dollars with a little help from a kid with a gang tat. It was the Bad Time all over again. It had been all I could do to keep my head together enough to come up with a new twist on my plan.

I looked in the mirror. After three years, Danny might look something like me. I tried the smirky little grin again, curling the right corner of my mouth and just lifting the upper lip on my left. That helped, especially with the shades and toque I'd asked Josh to get for me.

I didn't have to fool anyone for long. I didn't think I *would* fool anyone for long. I wasn't even sure if Josh believed me now. I'd said I didn't want them to meet at the shelter, because the little rooms were too much like where I'd been held for so long. I wanted to meet in a park, with lots of people and open space around us, so I could be calm. And so I could run like hell. All I had to do was get everyone confused enough for me to get a head start.

I pulled the little black brim on the toque back past my ear. I wondered how truly stupid it looked with Gap cargo shorts. I wondered if Josh was a fast runner. I flushed the toilet for show, then stepped into the hall, toeing out.

Josh was waiting, waggling keys to the shelter's van. He looked at me and grinned. "You know how hot it is out there, Danny?"

"This sucker is my look," I said from behind the shades. I was already getting tired of saying *sucker.* "Let's go."

The park was flat and open, cartoon green under sprinklers. I scoped an escape route around a fountain, through a playground and across the next parking lot. There were cars to dodge around and a sun-baked boulevard with a lot of traffic. Get across that, and then what? I guessed I'd find out.

Josh backed the van into a space at the edge of the lot and we sat there, waiting. There were only a few cars.

Apparently Tucsoners didn't go to the park when it was a hundred degrees out. My legs started bouncing.

"It's okay to be nervous," Josh said.

Tell me about it, I thought. I wondered again about him and running. The van doors were locked, and Josh had some kind of central control of them. I'd already tried mine when Josh was busy messing with the radio as we waited at a red light.

"There'll be a Canadian government person with her. From the consulate in LA. No police."

The air conditioner was on, but sweat prickled under my hat. I promised myself I'd dump it first chance I got. I wedged my hands under my legs to keep from fiddling with the door. I tried to breathe slowly and quit the bouncing, but I was fried. I'd only had a few hours' sleep, on top of everything that had happened. My brain was zapping around like a video game.

Then a white Focus with a rental-company sticker pulled up a little ways off. Two women got out. The one on the driver's side was small, with a frizz of blond hair above a beige jacket and skirt. She had flat shoes and a stylin' leather briefcase that Harley would have liked. The woman on the passenger side was chunky, in a yellow-and-orange-striped sundress that didn't make her look any smaller. She had tangled dark hair and a round, pale face behind oversized sunglasses. Her legs and feet were pale too, with red nail polish that matched her sandals. A white sweater was draped over a white shoulder bag.

"Here we go," Josh said. He popped the door locks. We climbed out. A chain-link fence ran along my side and behind us. There was nowhere to go but forward. I couldn't even do that: the heat slapped me harder than my first foster mother.

As I stood there, stunned, the women looked our way. The chunky one flinched. You could see her mouth, "Danny?" Then she screamed it, "DANNY!" and she skittered toward me, her sandals clacking on the pavement. Before I could move, she had grabbed me. I don't like it when people touch me.

"Danny." Now she was sobbing. She was all over me, and I couldn't move. It was awful. Finally, I lifted my hands on either side of her. It felt as if I was holding them out for the cuffs to be snapped on.

"Shan," I said. She didn't let go of me until the two of us were on a plane to Toronto.

FOUR

It was almost too easy. Shan was a motormouth. I could hardly keep up. She had photos with her of how the family looked now. "Just so they don't weird you out. Oh, Grampy looks frail, doesn't he? And he limps now. He had a stroke last year.

"Roy and the kids and I are in Port Hope now. I'm receptionist at the clinic and Roy's still at GM, thank God, even with the cutbacks. Brooklynne's going into grade one in September and Matt will be in grade five. Haven't they grown? Matt still remembers that time he got scared up on the big slide and you climbed up and pretended to be a monkey to get him down. He slides around in front of the TV just the way you used to. Sometimes I'll come in behind him and for a second I'll think it's you."

"Slides?" I fished. My voice sounded tight. I couldn't help it. Not only was this crazy, but I'd never been on a plane before.

"Oh, you know." Shan was still looking at the pictures. "How you used to put your hands flat on the floor and scoot around on your butt? I always thought it looked as if you were revving up to take off." She glanced over. "Oh God. Look at you. I'm sorry. I didn't mean you took off when all this...We know now *they* took you."

She hesitated a beat, then grabbed my hand, which was clutching the armrest. I pulled it back. I took a deep breath. "It's okay. It's just—" *Use the truth when you can. It's easier.* I looked at the seatback in front of me. There was a little TV screen there. "I don't like when people touch me. Because of..."

From the corner of my eye I saw her lips pinch in as she watched me. "Aw, hon. It was bad, I know. Josh told me about it."

I nodded and kept looking forward. "I don't want to talk about it."

"You don't have to."

I waited a second, and then I fished again. "Did you— did Momma—think..."

"That you ran off?" She looked at me hard. "Oh, hon. We were frantic. We didn't know what to think. And the police..." She closed her eyes. "They thought all kinds of things. They thought Da—I mean, *you*—" She flapped her hands around. "Oh God. Sorry, hon. It's been so long thinking…I'm having trouble getting my head around all this…Oh my God, never mind. Never mind what the police thought. Never mind any of it. It was awful. Never mind. You don't need to know."

"Know what?"

She shut her eyes and shook her head sharp and fast, as if she was trying to knock bad memories loose. Then she stopped and took a deep breath. Her voice went low and confidential, as if she was willing me to remember. "Listen, it wasn't always good at home. That's why you went to foster—to live with other families those two times. And it wasn't good, right before you…left. For anybody."

I nodded.

"Ty was way out of line, and he was scary, with his temper and the hitting. He hit you too—you don't have to pretend he didn't. And it was tough for you with Momma too. But you were younger then, and you were tough for her, being so wild and all. Okay? But after, when it got real bad…she blamed herself. She'd say it was all her fault and now Da—you were gone. She and Ty were both twisted up. Ty was just crazy after you disappeared. You might hear stuff about that. But you know what?" Shan's voice cracked. She fumbled a tissue out of her bag. "It made Momma stop drinking. No more drugs either. She's completely clean, sober, and Ty's way better too. He lives up in Peterborough. Isn't that great? And it's going to be way better now, because you're back. It's a fresh start for everybody." She was crying as she said it.

I nodded again. It really was all I could do just then because the plane was bumping around. I locked my eyes on the seatback screen. I was squeezing those armrests tight. When things settled down, I said, "I've never been on a plane before."

"Awww, sweetie, it's okay," she hiccupped through her tears. "When Roy and I took the kids to Orlando…"

I let her talk until she fell asleep. She'd told me she'd been up and rushing around ever since the phone call. I knew how she felt.

FIVE

I was tired too, but the feeling that something was wrong nagged at me. Like I said before, it felt almost too easy. Maybe I was just too wired, but when I was sure she was asleep, I went through Shan's shoulder bag. I didn't really know what I was looking for—it was habit, I guess. She had gum, tissues, makeup, a hairbrush, a pen, a chunky paperback called *Wild Haven,* sunglasses, tampons, headache pills, a newspaper page with a half-done Sudoku, a phone bill for 26 Yardley Street, Port Hope, ON, a wallet, her passport, the photo album.

Everything matched up. I took ten Canadian dollars from her wallet. She had over a hundred with her, so I figured she wouldn't notice right away. The bills were all different colors, like Monopoly money. *Never pass up a chance.* I wanted the birth certificate she'd shown for me at the airport—since Danny was fifteen, they'd said he didn't need a passport—but I left it for the time being. I stuffed the ten into a pocket of my shorts and turned to the pictures. The photo album was brand new. Shan said she'd put it together just for me. The pictures looked real. Why they would have been fake, I don't know. I was feeling pretty paranoid right then, and so tired I was getting mixed up.

I looked at Roy, muffin-topped in a golf shirt, arms around giggling kids; Gram and Grampy, perched in lawn chairs outside their RV in Florida. I half-wondered if I'd seen them. Harley and I had spent a month doing a charity-canvassing scam at seniors' RV parks down there last winter. There was skinny brother Tyson with a beer, a mullet and some bad tattoos. He looked like barbed wire in a T-shirt. Little momma Carleen looked about as huggable as a baseball bat, even in a Santa hat.

Whatever I was looking for, I didn't find it. Anyway, if Shan was the real deal, I couldn't see any reason why she'd be stringing me along. I put it all out of my head; I had enough to worry about. The seatback screen was showing a map of where we were in the flight. It wouldn't be long now—two hours at most. I flipped through the photos and looked into all those eyes. They hadn't seen Danny in three years. Could I fool them? *Any* of them? For how long? Long enough to figure out some kind of next move? What if Josh had figured it out and called ahead? What if cops were waiting? Would they check fingerprints? DNA?

I closed my eyes. *Don't overthink.* What choice did I have? It was this or the Bad Time. Sooner or later, I was going to have to run. I could hit the ground running. Yeah, if it wasn't snowing up there in Canada, I could always run.

SIX

I must've slept, because I felt a bump and then we were landing. It was sunset. It wasn't snowing. It was summer. There were no cops, no questions, no calls from Josh. I felt like glass. At Immigration, I snagged Danny's birth certificate when they handed it back. "S'okay. Sucker's mine, right? I'll feel safer." I stuffed it into the same pocket as the money and jammed on my shades. We moved toward a sign that said *CUSTOMS*. Past it were blank sliding glass doors. Past them was anybody's guess. I was ready to run. Shan grabbed my hand as we stepped through the doors. As I tried to shake her off, I heard "There!" People rushed us. I yelled and spun away, but Shan held tight. I flailed at her. Then I was drowning in people.

"Oh my GOD!"

"…thought we'd see the day…"

"…hoped and prayed…"

It was the family. Later I saw the pictures. They were carrying a Welcome Home banner. I had a sort-of smile that looked as if it had been glued to my teeth. I'd thought I'd shatter every time someone grabbed me.

The laughing, clapping, crying died down. Someone—Grampy, maybe—called out, "Let him talk! Danny. Whaddya got to say?"

I didn't know if I could talk. I opened my mouth. Out came "Let's eat."

They laughed like they'd fall over.

"Whaddya feel like, tiger?" said a guy who was probably Uncle Pete.

"Wings," I said. "What else?"

They laughed again.

Dinner at Boston Pizza went easy. No one asked too much. Mostly I said I was tired, which was true, kept my head down and listened hard. The only tricky bit came when we all sat down. I wasn't passing up a free meal, but I'd made sure to take a chair that gave me an easy getaway. By then, I'd done some mental matching with the picture album. People were missing. I knew I had to ask.

"Hey," I said. "Where's Momma? And Ty?"

For a second no one answered. Then Uncle Pete said, "They couldn't get off work. Ty's up at General Packaging. And your mom is at the new grocery in Cobourg. What's it called?"

"Green Leaf," Gram said.

"She's on steady nights, hon," Shan said. "You'll be staying with us for the time being. We don't want you being alone."

"Bummer," I said. Then, "I mean, about them not being here." They laughed *again*. I couldn't believe it. I was starting to feel like a comedian.

By the time we hit the highway, I was beginning to wonder if I might just pull it off. Not forever, just long enough to get some money and make a plan. Danny would be sixteen on November 9. No one could come after me then. What if I slipped away into the States, left a note saying I loved them all but was just too messed up? Rolling along now, watching *Cars* with the kids on the DVD player in the van, I remembered one of the photos. It was of a younger, slimmer Shan, her arms around a skinny little Danny in soccer shorts. They were smiling, squinting into the sun, happy. All at once I got this power surge. I *was* going to pull it off. Know why? Because they wanted me to. I was making them happy. *Feeling good is what we sell.* If they wanted Danny, I'd give them Danny. Maybe I'd be happy too. I almost laughed at that. Maybe I did, because Shan turned around and winked at me. It was almost as if she knew what I was thinking.

SEVEN

Harley took me from the Bad Time. He got me from Barbie and Ken, the Bible thumpers. This was up in Portland, Oregon, where I was a ward of the state from the time I was born. They were something like my eighteenth family. The Bad Time is what I call the swamp that stretches back to before I can remember. People from then bubble up in dreams sometimes. The cardigan-sweater lady who baked cookies and hit me if I didn't show her everything I did in the toilet. The cheery chubbies who made me wear their fat kids' old clothes and spent my support allowance on a game system I wasn't allowed to use. The neat freaks who threw away all my books because they cluttered the room I was supposed to keep tidy. The accountants with matching glasses—he liked to come to my room to "talk" on nights when she'd taken a sleeping pill.

Not everyone was bad. *I* was bad. Or maybe I became bad. After a while I didn't wait for anyone to mess with me—I messed with *them*. Anyway, the thumpers weren't the worst and they weren't the best. They weren't really called Ken and Barbie either. Wayne and Patti were their names. I think they wanted to be Ken and Barbie though. They'd come up from some Bible college in California. They had shiny teeth, and we prayed a lot when they weren't watching Fox News or trying to save me and the gay tree huggers. Wayne and Patti thought gay stuff was the worst sin going— that and jerking off.

"Keep yourself clean," Wayne would warn. "Never sin against yourself. There are real fires, literal fires of hell, and they burn. Give me your left hand."

Then he'd hold my hand over a red-hot stove element—not touching it, but I didn't know he wouldn't. I'd try to pull away, but he was stronger than me and I'd feel him pushing my hand closer and closer. The first time, I was so scared I wet myself. I got in trouble for that too. It was always my left hand Wayne did the stove thing with. I didn't tell him I used my right. Instead I'd go into the bathroom and do it all over his toothbrush first chance I got. Then I'd get in a fight at school.

The main problem with Wayne and Patti was the churchgoing and having to pray out loud for forgiveness when I got in trouble, which was a lot. That and the sucker punching to the kidneys. I wasn't kidding about

Bible *thumpers.* I guess the Bible said hitting was okay, but the state didn't like bruises.

Harley had been with Darla then, doing their Bill and Bonnie Blessing ministry number. They came through Wayne and Patti's church. Harley said getting me was easy. He told them to wait a day and then say I'd run off. It wouldn't have been the first time I'd run.

For a long time, I thought Harley had paid them for me. I asked him once a couple of years later, just to know what I was worth. "Give me a fucking break," he said. "They paid *me.*" His voice went all singsongy. "*A small offering unto the Lord that we might take this child under our wings on the path to salvation.*" He snorted and popped a fresh piece of gum. "I'll guarantee you, they didn't pay me as much as the next foster-allowance check, and they didn't report you missing until they'd cashed it. You must have been a royal pain in the ass."

"I didn't pray loud enough before meals."

"Chew with your mouth closed is all I ask."

I don't remember much about how I felt when Wayne told me to get into Harley and Darla's RV with my green garbage bag of clothes. The RV had *BLESSINGS TO YOU* painted on its side in sky blue. I'm sure I figured it couldn't be any worse than staying where I was, and anyway, back then I was super good at not letting myself feel things.

I remember sitting in the back of the RV, watching Darla crack her window and light a smoke when we went around the corner. When we stopped at the first traffic light, Harley said around his gum, "Hey kid, grab me a beer from the fridge back there."

He popped it open, still watching the road. "What are we gonna call you, anyway?"

I didn't say anything.

"Bill Junior." Darla blew smoke out the window. "That way, there's no screwups."

"Work for you?" Harley glanced at me over his shoulder. I nodded and went back and sat down. The only thing that surprised me about any of it was being asked. I knew they were supposed to be traveling preachers, but I was way past expecting anyone to be what they said they were. Even Wayne had had a porn stash behind some paneling in the basement. I'd left it spread all over the family room with a note that said *left or right?* before they called me upstairs to go with Harley and Darla. I'm good at finding things.

I remember liking that we had KFC and Dr. Pepper for dinner in the RV that first night. Nobody said grace either. In the Bad Time I'd gotten things like mashed potatoes and minute steak with water or milk—except with the fit freaks. With them, it was all tofu, brown rice, fish and steamed vegetables. That was even worse.

After dinner, Darla lit another smoke. Harley belched and said, "Oh baby, that hit the spot." It was better than praying and stove elements, but it didn't mean I trusted them. I kept a steak knife from the kitchenette drawer under the mattress for the first few months. They never bothered me that way though; they didn't even do it with each other much. Mostly it was just business.

That was what they'd gotten me for: Business. At first I was just cover for them—everybody trusts a family more. I was small for my age and I looked younger than I was, especially after they got me some new clothes and a haircut. "Stand beside me and smile. Then give them an envelope. Say 'Blessings to you.'"

"Blessings to you."

"You're a natural. You like school?" Harley worked his gum.

I shrugged. I hated school.

"Well, we move around a lot. This is a different school. School of life. Right now we're going to work this mall. Smile and hold Darla's hand when we walk."

That was the only part I didn't like, but I managed.

Harley pulled the door open. "Everything you need to know, you're going to learn from us. Keep your ears and eyes open."

EIGHT

You'd better believe my eyes and ears were open now. I didn't know squat about Canada or the town of Port Hope, except that Shan and Roy and the kids lived in a semi (whatever that was) at 26 Yardley Street. A semi turned out to mean "semidetached": the place was joined up to a twin house on one side. It was the kind of neighborhood Harley might have run his vinyl-siding-refresher scam in, or sent me through selling phony magazine subscriptions to "raise money for my school." I wasn't expected to know anything, though, because they'd moved from their old town. The one I "disappeared" from. When Shan asked, I said I didn't want to go back or see anyone from there, because it brought back bad memories.

Everything seemed completely straight up. In some ways, it was a pretty standard game. I came up with memories for Uncle Pete that I got from Gram and memories for Grampy that I got from Uncle Pete. I toed out. I used the word *sucker* a lot. I scooted back and forth on my butt beside Matt and Brooklynne when we watched TV. (It was tiring; maybe Danny had ADHD.) I must have been a pretty good Danny Dellomondo, because they bought it. You could tell by the way Gram and Grampy hugged me before they headed back to their place in Havelock, about an hour's drive north. Shan told me I had a case worker assigned from Children's Aid to help "facilitate my transitioning." She was going to come by in a couple of days, but right now I could just chill.

It was easy for her to say. For the first time in three years I'd stopped moving, but my brain was still going flat-out, bouncing around as if I were trapped on a bumper car ride. It was hard to take a breath, especially in a little house with four strangers who were supposed to be my family. We were watching each other all the time and pretending we weren't. When Shan said Matt wanted to show me around town, I didn't know if he did or not, but I let him. It was a chance to stretch, scope an exit and pump a little more info.

At first, I'd thought Port Hope was like a lot of towns in the northeastern States. Then I'd started noticing differences, like everything was in kilometers and liters, not miles and gallons. That took me awhile to figure out. And there were one- and two-dollar coins instead of bills. Also, there was foreign printing on packages, in what turned out to be French. I didn't get why, because nobody in the town spoke it as far as I could tell, but of course I couldn't ask. I was just worried that I'd be expected to know. One day, looking at a cereal box, I'd said, "I forgot about this being on everything. I can't even read it."

"Well, join the club," Shan said. "We're thinking about French immersion for Brooklynne, but I don't know." That hadn't helped. After I'd found the library, I read newspapers until I learned about Quebec, this place in Canada that was all French.

I found the library the day Matt showed me around. The main street ran up and down a hill. A river crossed it at the bottom, running out to a lake. There were a lot of people around, and touristy shops selling expensive crap for your kitchen and whatever. You could almost hear the money crinkle. Harley would have had four games worked out before he parked.

It was hot. Not Tucson hot, but muggy. Matt was wearing a cap with *NY* on the front. He wheeled along beside me, straddling his little tricks bike. I'd ditched my rapper cap but kept my shades on.

Matt didn't have much to say except that he liked Xbox better than Game Boy but he really wanted a Wii. He was saving up but hoped Grampy would help. I wondered if Matt kept his money in his room. It would be worth a look.

It was too early to pump him about the family, so I worked on exits. Which way is the highway, where's the lake, how big is it, what's there, what's on the other side? A lot of it, he didn't even know. You could tell he was bored. He kept circling back on the bike and trying to jump the curb. I finally got lucky when I asked, "What's that place?"

"Uh, the library."

"Let's go in," I said. It popped out before I could stop myself.

"What for?" Matt curled up one side of his mouth and pulled his chin in as if he was scared it would get contaminated. I recognized the Danny smirk I'd been practicing. I guessed it ran in the family.

"I don't know," I said. "Get a book."

Matt waggled his front wheel. "Why? It's summer."

"I know. And it's hot. And it'll be air-conditioned."

"Let's just go get a pop."

By now I knew "pop" was what they called sodas in Canada. I gave him back the smirk. "Got any money?"

"No," Matt said. "Do you?"

"Come in there with me," I said, "and I'll get us some."

Now he looked at me. "How?"

"You'll see." All at once I was doing a Harley: I was seeing three moves ahead, and it felt good. I knew Matt couldn't resist. He put his bike in the rack. We walked into the cool.

NINE

The way I figured it was this: First, I *did* need a book—and bad—to slow down my head. I'd always been a reader. I had to be. In the Bad Time, it was sometimes the only way for me to escape. TV was always the first thing they took from you when you messed up. Second, I had Shan's ten in my pocket, but I had to have a way I'd gotten the money. If Matt told Shan I had ten dollars in Canadian money with me, she was going to wonder where it had come from and maybe check her purse. Nobody was going to believe I'd gotten it in Tucson. The library was perfect. All I had to do was brush against somebody or bump a purse, then flash the ten at Matt, and he'd think I'd picked someone's pocket. If he was in on it, he couldn't tell Shan. I'd be an outlaw superhero and he'd be an accessory. *It's all about leverage.*

Inside, there was a three-sided counter with a lady behind it and scanner bars to walk through on the way out. I could see a kids' section and stairs leading up to the rest of the library. "Come on," I said to Matt.

Upstairs was another desk with another lady, public computers and books. Tons of books.

I felt myself relax a little. Man, if I could just hang here by myself, I thought. One of my worst times was when the neat freaks threw away my books. That might have been the last time I cried. There was one book I loved, about this girl named Gilly. She was a Bad Timer like me. She was great at messing with people's heads. The difference was, she had a mom, and even a picture of her, but the mom turned out to be a shit, and Gilly had to get it together for herself anyway. Me and Gilly. I loved that there wasn't a happy ending, even though she had a grandma. I would have been so pissed if she'd gotten out and I hadn't.

"Just go with this," I whispered to Matt. All at once I had to be alone in there, just for a minute.

"Can I help you boys?"

The lady at the desk had a name badge that said *Jo-Anne* and MOM stamped on her forehead. I jumped right into it. I nodded at Matt. "Well, ma'am, he'd like to use a computer and I'd like to look at the books." Matt stared at me. I didn't care. Sticking Matt at a computer would give me time to breathe and steal a couple books. Then I could fake stealing the money.

"Do you have cards?" the lady smiled.

I looked at Matt. He did the family look again. It was starting to bug me. I didn't let him see that, though, because I'd just realized something else: someone was offering me more ID. "No, ma'am," I said. "I'm new in town."

"Well, welcome," said Jo-Anne. "Anyone over thirteen can get their own card, but I'll need to see something with your address. Do you have anything with you?"

I looked at Matt. He shrugged and did the stupid smirk again. "I guess not, ma'am," I said. I decided to steal the little jerk's Wii money for sure.

"That's okay." Jo-Anne smiled again. "I can do a temporary sign-up for the computer, but you can't take any books out until you get a card. You'll have to come back for that." She pointed behind her. "There's a computer free over in the teen section."

I nodded back. "Yes, ma'am. Thank you, we'll do that. Can I still look around though?"

"Oh, sure. Take your time. If you find something you really want, they'll hold it for you at the desk downstairs."

"That would be super, ma'am."

Jo-Anne turned to Matt and asked his name. I nudged him forward, then headed into the book stacks, fast. Matt wouldn't last very long. I grabbed a few paperbacks. I'd leave some at the desk and come back for a card, but I needed at least one for now.

Boosting books from a library is not exactly hard, especially when you have big pockets in your cargo shorts.

I ducked into the second-last aisle for a quiet spot where I could find the sensor stickers and tear them out and almost ran into one of those rolling carts they move books around on. A tall skinny girl in jeans and a sweater was sticking books back on a top shelf. We both kind of jumped. She had long mousy hair and ugly glasses and a name badge. She stared at me. I wheeled around and ducked down the last aisle instead. I found the sensors. When I heard her roll the book cart away, I ripped out the pages they were stuck on and slipped the two smallest books in my pockets. Then I went to run the fake theft.

There were a bunch of old folks I could bump into, but I wanted Matt watching. Then I looked down the stairs and saw a chance to get more money. At the checkout, the clerk was opening a cash drawer under the counter with a little key. Somebody was saying, "I've got five photocopies." I looked around, saw the photocopier over near Jo-Anne, and it all just fell into place.

I palmed the ten-dollar bill, then went and got Matt. He followed me as I went to the copier and grabbed a sheet of paper from the wastebasket. I gave it to him. "Hold this, stand by the stairs and watch me."

I started walking away from Matt, my head down. I bobbled the books I was carrying in front of me as if I was busy looking at them and bumped into a guy. There was no way I was really going to pick his pocket—I'm not good enough. Harley was pretty good at it, and he'd started teaching me, but not even he did it unless we really

had to. Then I'd just be the stall while he was the mechanic.
Now all I did was apologize and walk back to Matt.
I flashed the ten in my hand and we started downstairs.

"How'd you do that?" Matt whispered.

"Never mind. I had to learn it. Now, c'mon."

I led him to the kids' section. "Grab five big books."

"Why?"

"*Never mind.* Just do it." I was getting really tired
of Matt.

We took all the books to the desk. I balanced them
there in a stack.

The lady there was no bigger than me. Her name tag
said *Daphne.* "We need to come back to get cards, ma'am,
but Jo-Anne upstairs said you could hold these for us."

"Absolutely," Daphne said. She looked at us over
those half-glasses. I told her our names and address and
she wrote it all down on a slip of paper. She was quick,
like a bird, which was not good. I decided to go for
it anyway. Before she could touch the stack of books,
I said, "Oh, and we have to pay for a photocopy." Matt
was still holding the sheet of paper. I passed Daphne
the ten. As she opened the cash drawer to make change,
I tipped over the books. They hit the floor on her side
of the counter. "Oh, sorry!"

She went for the books. I leaned over the counter like
I was trying to help. Instead, I slipped the first bill I could
reach out of the drawer and scooped it behind my back
to Matt. Then I ran around to help for real. As I did,

the tall girl from upstairs came to the desk. I was pretty sure she hadn't seen what I'd done. I kept my back to her. She didn't say a word.

We got the books gathered up again. Daphne gave me change from my ten for the photocopy. It had cost a quarter.

When we got outside, Matt was bug-eyed. I said, "How much did we get?"

"Five dollars." His voice was shaky. He started to reach into his pocket.

"Not here! Get your bike."

He pulled his bike out of the rack, and we crossed the street into a park. I pulled the books I'd boosted out of my pockets. Matt's eyes got even bigger. "Okay," I said, "so we made five plus nine seventy-five...Wait." I put the books down on a picnic table under a tree. I fished the money out of my pocket and dumped it on the table. The Canadian five was blue, and there were a couple of those weird two-dollar coins. The ten had been purple. I pushed it all toward him.

"What're you doing?" Matt said.

"You helped," I said. "You did great. So we're partners. You won't tell, right? 'Cause if you do, we're screwed. Can I trust you?"

"Y-yeah. Sure," Matt stammered.

"And to show I trust you, I'm going to let you hold it for us. You got a secret place at home where you keep your money safe?"

He nodded.

"How much you got?"

"Twenty-eight bucks."

"Good. Plus this. Put it all there. But you got to show me where it is, so I'll know you haven't skimmed it. Okay?"

"Okay." He stuffed the cash in his pocket. His hands were trembling.

"Cool. I guess we got money for drinks, huh? See why I like going to the library? And believe me, your mom will like it that we went there too." I picked up the books. I was feeling good. Thanks to Matt, who'd be too scared to talk, I now had a hiding place for cash, ID on the way and books. Matt didn't know it yet, but he'd just donated his twenty-eight bucks to my escape fund too.

As we went to the variety store, there was only one thing niggling at me. The tall girl in the library: as we were leaving, I'd seen her name tag. I could've sworn it read *Gilly*.

TEN

Roy went back to work the next day. Shan took the kids to dentist appointments that afternoon. She was all worried about leaving me alone. I was dying for them to go.

"Are you sure, hon? We won't be long. They're booking a checkup for you for next week. I tried for today, but they're full up."

"I just wanna read." I waved a library book.

"Well, you've got my cell number, right?"

As soon as they were gone, I went through the house, top to bottom. Like I said, it was an old habit.

Roy had a couple of joints in a cigarette pack in the back of his sock drawer. Shan had underwear that surprised me, and in one of her winter boots there was $187, a bunch of it in those one- and two-dollar coins.

That, plus the money Matt showed me in the bottom of the Lego box, was an excellent start for my escape fund. Then I hit another jackpot: a stack of old home DVDs. I started watching them. When they all got back from the dentist, it was after four. I told Shan I'd make dinner. I'd already checked the kitchen, and there was stuff for spaghetti.

"Really?"

"I used to have to cook sometimes," I said. It was true. After Darla left, Harley kept the RV for a while. Later on we stayed as much as we could in places with kitchenettes, because it was cheaper. He said it was healthier too. Whenever we could cook, Harley would claim he'd gone off junk food after his carncy days. Then he'd get me to help him make stuff. We only ever made a few things, like spaghetti or tacos or chili, and then we'd downgrade to KD and frozen fish sticks, and then we'd be back to KFC or pizza.

It was a hot, sticky afternoon. The house didn't have central air. Shan sat by the kitchen door, sipping from a tin of iced tea and watching Brooklynne in her blow-up wading pool. I dumped ground beef in the frypan. As it began to sizzle, I said, "Know what this reminds me of? Remember the time I tried to make Momma a birthday cake?"

"Oh God, yeah. What were you—nine, ten?"

I shrugged. The answer was ten—I'd checked the date/time stamp at the bottom of the DVD screen—

but you don't always want to be too accurate; it can look suspicious.

Shan started to giggle. "There was flour everywhere, remember? And Toby got into it…"

Toby was a dog. I still didn't know what had happened to him. "Yeah, and there were balloons or something."

"Right. God, I'd forgotten." She looked at me like she was stunned "How did—"

I shrugged. "Some stuff just sticks, you know?"

She nodded slowly and looked back to Brooklynne. "You know, I think I even recorded that. I've got that somewhere. We transferred everything to DVD. I'll look after dinner." I didn't tell her it was third from the bottom in the left-hand pile. "We should eat outside, it's so hot," Shan said. "The big saucepan is down there."

I found it and turned on the tap.

"God, this is so sweet of you," she went on. "Listen, Danny, Meg from Children's Aid called me today. She's coming tomorrow to meet you. And Monday afternoon the police will be here. They just need to get a statement. She said not to worry, that she'd be with you for that."

Something must have shown on my face, because Shan said, "I'm going to come home early so I can be here too."

ELEVEN

kind of liked Meg. You could tell she was new enough to the job that she didn't have her whole Bad Time vibe happening yet—or maybe my just being "poor Danny" made her switch it off. Either way, she was young and very hot, with long dark hair and shiny nails. Best of all, she never questioned anything I said. I think she liked it best when I didn't say anything and just looked hurt or small or whatever. Her favorite thing to say was "We all want to make this work." She said TV reporters and newspapers had been calling her office about me, and she'd deal with them if we wanted her to. "I'll just say that it's a private family time and that everybody is relieved and happy that you're home."

There were two cops, Swofford and Griffin. Swofford was a young guy with a cue-ball head, all steroids and golf clothes. Griffin was a bag of cement. Gray every-thing—sloppy suit, hair, tie, clipped moustache. Even his eyes were gray. The cops made Shan's little front room feel even smaller. Meg perched on the stool that went with Brooklynne and Matt's electric keyboard. You could see down her top when she leaned forward. Shan sat on the couch beside me. I could feel her wanting to hold my hand. Swofford had a chair from the kitchen. Griffin slumped in Roy's recliner like he owned the place.

Constable Swofford had a little voice recorder and took notes. Griffin was a detective sergeant. "Retired, actually," he said. He even had a cement voice. "But I handled your case when you disappeared. Wanted to see it wrapped up. Hope you don't mind." He asked Shan how she was, said he hadn't seen her in a long time. She gave him a tight, one-millisecond smile. When he asked about Ty, she didn't even give him that.

"He's fine." Good, I thought. Cops brought the Bad Time with them like crap on their shoes. I didn't want Shan tight with them. *Your enemy's enemy is your friend.*

Then Meg said, "We all want to make this work."

Swofford clicked his pen and started the recorder. I gave them the same line I'd fed Josh.

Two guys in a white van offered me a ride. They gave me a drink—it must have had drugs in it. When I woke up I was in the place they kept me for a long time. There were other boys there too. Mostly everyone spoke a foreign language, Spanish maybe. The suckers changed the way we looked. They injected my eyes with something. Men came there and we had to do things for them. They kept us on drugs. We weren't supposed to talk. The windows were barred and we weren't allowed out, except to go in this little yard where it was always hot. A few months ago I escaped when a door was left open. I tried to get far away. I didn't go to the police because I thought some of the men at the place I got away from were police. I don't know how far I got. I didn't even know where I was when the guy who died in the parking lot saw me. He said his name was Bill. He said he'd bring me up to Canada if I helped him do some stuff along the way, like what we were doing with the pin machines. I knew that was shady, but Bill said if I told the cops I'd go to jail too. I had to do what he said and hope I could get close enough to home to get away.

That was it. Simple. I talked low, looking away from the cops. Every so often I'd stop, as if it was too much for me. That part wasn't hard: it almost *was* too much for me. The story had worked with Josh, but even he might not have believed all of it. He'd believed I was Danny, though, and that was what counted. Cops listen differently. Swofford nodded and wrote. Griffin just slouched until I got to the part about my eyes. Then he said, "That must have hurt."

I nodded. "It was bad. I don't like to remember."

"What about your hands, Danny?" Griffin asked. "Did they do anything to your hands?"

Swofford looked up from his notebook.

I looked down at my hands. What was this about? Did he mean altering fingerprints? Harley had said he'd heard about guys trying to do that. If that's what Griffin meant, he might be accidentally feeding me a big out. One I could use if they ever checked me against Danny's prints—if they had them. It also meant he was buying my story. I wanted to scream *"YES!"* but I had to play it like everything else. *It's not what you say, it's how you say it.* I looked back up at him "I-I don't know. It's hazy from, like, the drugs. I think I remember them being wrapped up, but I thought that was so I couldn't grab anything or try to escape."

"Hmm," Griffin said, staring at me. "We got some latent prints from your house after you disappeared. They're in the file."

My heart started revving. All I could do was look back at him and shrug.

There was a silence like glue. Then he shifted his bulk. The chair creaked and the mood snapped. "The prints are useless. Too faint. Till puberty really kicks in, there's not enough oil in a kid's skin for a print to last more than a few hours." He slowly shook his gray head. "Eye color. God. When they find a way to mess with DNA, we're done."

Shan hugged me. "Well, nobody tampered with this guy's DNA," she said. "He's just the same as he always was."

I almost hugged her back.

Next, they asked a bunch of questions about Harley. I told the truth about where we'd been for the last while because it was too easy to check. When it was over, Swofford flipped his notebook shut and turned off his recorder and said he was glad I was back. He said he'd bring me a statement to sign for the files and that they'd be in touch with the FBI, who might want to talk to me too.

We all stood up. Meg bent to pick up her shoulder bag. I got another look down her top. Swofford looked too; I saw him. Griffin said, "Good to meet you."

I nodded.

"We rarely get a happy ending." He cocked a gray eyebrow. "Stay safe, huh?"

Stay away from you, I thought.

TWELVE

After the cops left, I relaxed a little. It felt like Shan did too. Maybe she was just getting used to having me around. Now the only ones I hadn't met were Danny's mom, Carleen, and his half-brother, Tyson. Peterborough, where Tyson lived, was half an hour north, but he'd had his license suspended for DUI. He'd also had his car repo'd. It didn't look like he was going to be much of a player.

Carleen, though, she was another story. I knew she was close by. Shan kept saying she'd be coming over soon. A couple times I heard Shan talking on the phone, and I got the feeling she was talking to Carleen. I don't know why exactly—just an edge in her voice that put *me* on edge. For a whole week Carleen didn't show. At first I worried that it was weird, a mother not coming to see her long-lost kid. Then I remembered Shan had said that things had been bad between Carleen and Danny before he disappeared, and that she'd been pretty messed up back then. Maybe she was worried about what *I* was going to do or say. Besides, what did I know about mothers? Whoever my mother was, visiting wasn't at the top of her list either. Finally, I decided not to worry about it. As long as Carleen wasn't around, she was one less person to fool.

I'd gone to the library a couple more times and gotten my card. I wanted to see if I could find that girl again. I just couldn't believe I'd seen *Gilly* on her name tag. It became a kind of good-luck thing for me. I thought if I could see the name and it was *Gilly*, then it would be some kind of sign that somehow things were going to work out all right. I couldn't get it out of my mind.

Harley could be like that too—watching for signs that his luck was running. He'd glued a little tourist-shop carving of a totem pole on the dash. He'd reach over, tap it and say, "Touch wood" any time he was talking about how a deal should go. Other times, though, when he'd had a few beers or when he saw people lined up to buy lottery tickets, he'd start in on how there was no such thing as luck. "Luck is what you make for yourself," he'd say. "Luck didn't buy this watch." Then he'd flash his big silver watch at me. Which was kind of funny, because Harley was right. Luck hadn't bought it, he had, for ten bucks from a bald guy named Charlie, who'd had a gym bag full of fake Rolexes and Tag Heuers. I'd been with him. Sometimes Harley could get so into it that he'd forget what was a scam and what was real. Maybe that's what made him so good.

Whatever her name was, the girl never showed up at the library. I told myself that was okay, that it didn't mean I'd read the tag wrong. As long as I didn't know for sure, my luck was still holding.

Another thing about the library was, it was the perfect place to get away from everybody. With Harley I'd been like a con-game sprinter; now it was starting to feel as if I were running a marathon.

The getaway part backfired, of course. Shan was impressed that I liked books. "It's so great," she said. I was lazing on Roy's recliner, which was a no-no. I knew Roy was also ticked about how much hot water I used. "Reading was such a problem for you. Remember how you used to hate it?" She was always saying stuff like that to me. *Remember how* and *remember when* or, holding something up, *remember this?* Sometimes I wondered if she was testing me, sometimes it was almost like she was coaching me. But I only thought like that when I was really uptight. Mostly it felt as if she just wanted someone to remember with her. It made her happy. That was my job, to make her happy.

Anyway, I wasn't surprised to hear about Danny not reading, and it was easy to handle. "There was no TV," I said. "Just a bunch of old books. I didn't have any choice. Now it's a habit, I guess."

"Good," she said. "I hope it rubs off on Matt." Then came the catch. "Listen, do you think you could take Brooklynne to the library? I haven't got time, and it would be so good for her."

What could I say? I took Brooklynne. She wanted me to read to her. It wasn't so bad; I like little-kid books. I don't remember anyone ever reading to me, so it was like I was reading for myself too.

When we came back to the house, we went around to the backyard. Shan was standing in the wading pool. In front of her, smoking a cigarette, was a skinny woman in denim cutoffs and a sleeveless yellow top. She had a tattoo of a dragon or something twisting up one arm. It sounded as if they were arguing, but they cut it off and turned when they heard us. Shan's face was red.

"Gramma," Brooklynne said.

So this was Carleen.

I used to have a dream about my mom. She was dark-haired, young and pretty, but still mom-looking. She'd have on a hair band and a blue gingham shirt and jeans, and she'd be smiling as she served me pancakes. I held on to that until the day I saw her doing the same thing on TV to a gap-toothed kid with freckles and realized I'd been rerunning a syrup commercial in my sleep.

For a while after that, I figured my mom was more likely a crack whore and probably dead. I wasn't even sure what a crack whore was, but it sounded like the worst thing you could be, and that had to be her. Otherwise, why wouldn't she come get me? Then I made her into someone more exotic who *couldn't* get to me, or didn't know about me. A cool spy who couldn't risk blowing her cover because her family would be in danger, or an heiress who'd had me when she was sixteen and whose evil family gave me away and told her I'd died, but she'd always kept a baby picture of me and one day she'd find me and take me home and I'd be rich.

Carleen wasn't any of those things. She was thin-faced, with streaked blond hair, pinched lips and eyes like bruises. Harley would have said she looked as if she'd gone ten rounds with the world. All *I* could say was, "Momma."

Carleen's whole body stiffened. She jammed her cigarette to her lips and sucked hard. Then she threw the butt away and stepped toward me, shakily blowing smoke as if she were the dragon on her own arm. "Danny."

Up close, I could smell weed under the tobacco. I still had my shades on. I wasn't much taller than she was. She clutched at her tattooed arm and twitched a smile together. Her eyes were flat and glassy as she stared at Bart Simpson's face on a T-shirt I'd borrowed from Matt. "It's been…It's…it's gr—it's good…it's…"

You could tell she didn't like hugging any better than I did, but she started for it, then stopped halfway and just held onto my arms. "Lissen." She gave me a little shake, still staring at Bart. "Lissen, um, sorry I haven't, ah, been *by*, but there's been things, you know. Life, like." She shot a look back at Shan. "But now...you're here."

"It's good to be back," I said.

"Are you?" she said. She finally looked at me. It was the blankest look I've ever seen. It was as if she wasn't behind her own eyes. At the time, I put it down to the weed and whatever else she was on. I'd been on a winning streak, and I'd started to think I could handle anything the Dellomondos threw at me. Maybe I was wrong.

THIRTEEN

Shan wanted Carleen to go clothes shopping with us. School was coming up soon, and I needed stuff. I'd ditched the hip-hop hat, but otherwise I'd been stuck with what I had worn on the plane and Matt's clothes when I had to. His stuff ran to Simpsons or camo T-shirts and twenty-times-too-large basketball shorts, which are fine if you're a moose hunter or Shaquille O'Neal but not so great on me. They weren't so great on Matt, either, but I didn't tell him.

With Harley, there were always lots of clothes. You had to dress for whatever line you were running. "Clothes make the man," I read to him one day.

"Correction," he'd said back. "Clothes make the scam."

If we were working RV parks, we'd dress Walmart or Penney's. Upscale, it depended—either designer labels or preppy stuff like J. Press or Brooks Brothers. Price didn't matter, since Harley always paid with juiced cards. We'd boost lots of things, usually things you could resell, but not often clothes. For a little while we were heavy into that, because store security never paid much attention to an okay-dressed kid and his dad. I was a walking disguise. We stopped, though, after a husband-and-wife shoplifting team got splashed all over the news for going on one of those trash-talk TV shows and bragging about how they boosted stuff using their little kids for cover.

Now we piled into the family van and went to Walmart and Zellers, which was like the same thing, only Canadian. I hear it's Target now. I wondered if it was the same mall Danny had wanted to go to when he disappeared. Driving there, I was tempted to say, "So, I finally get to go to the mall with you after all," but I kept my mouth shut. It wasn't a Danny thing to say, and I still needed to play it right with Carleen, whether she was stoned or not.

At the mall, I updated Danny. I picked black jeans and a pair of distressed ones, a couple plain gray tops and a striped shirt that buttoned up tight. With socks and under-wear, they'd spent their limit. While Shan and Carleen talked to some friend they'd bumped into, I strolled behind a rack of shiny dress pants and boosted some tight black T-shirts to help out. It took about five seconds to lay one flat inside a gray top and fold one into the black jeans.

I was rusty. I remembered to check for scanner trig-gers on the tees, but I hadn't scoped out the cameras when we walked in. A security guard stopped us at the till. I said I didn't do it, didn't know how the shirts got there. Meg got called. I had to wait in a little room while she straightened it out.

I know we all want this to work.

Through the door I heard her telling Shan and Carleen that this was a "normal trauma indicator" and it showed how stressed I'd been. The store manager even gave me one of the T-shirts when he found out my sad story. I didn't tell him I was still wearing a third one I'd slipped on in the change room.

In a weird way, I think getting caught like that was a winner. It looked like exactly the kind of bonehead play Danny would have made. It matched right up with my lasting an hour in high school the next week.

FOURTEEN

Not that I'd planned on being there much. I hadn't been in a school since grade six in Oregon. I'd hated it then and I didn't see why it would be any different now.

Meg had put me in a remedial class until they figured out what grade I could handle and how well I would socialize. There had been stuff in the news about Danny being found. The local and Toronto papers had called. A TV crew had interviewed Meg and Shan and Swofford, but they'd all been kept away from me, so there were no new photos or anything, even though they said we lived in Port Hope now. Stories had gotten around, I guess. Anyway, I was at my new locker when I heard snickering and feet shuffling right behind me. Someone said, "You really blow all those guys?"

Usually, there are three of them. I went with that now. The main thing, no matter how many there are, is to move first and keep moving, so I just wheeled and smacked the closest guy in the face with my new math book. Which made it good for something. As the kid's head snapped back, I kicked him as hard as I could, right where it counts, and piled on as he crumpled. When you're my size, you hit first and hope someone breaks it up before you get hit back.

It worked in grade six and it worked now. By the time the yelling started, I had him on the floor, hitting him anywhere I could, and a few seconds later some teacher was dragging me off and I was on my way to the office. I wouldn't talk to anybody until Meg got there. When she did, looking hot in sandals and a summer dress, we all wanted to make it work, so the next day I started at Open Book, the "alternative" school.

I liked Open Book. It was just a room over the Big Sisters secondhand store downtown, about a block from the library—everything in Port Hope was close. It had tables and chairs and bookshelves, and sometimes even some students. For assignments, you filled in workbooks. The teacher, Mr. Hunter, was a short head-shaved guy who wore jogging shoes with relaxed-fit khakis and polyester dress shirts. He kept his car keys in the pocket of the jacket he always draped across the back of his chair. I knew that by the second day.

Mr. Hunter was happy if you showed up. The girls usually brought their babies with them. The guys were hip-hop hillbillies, skinny stoners with wallets on chains and bad everything. Mostly what they did was take smoke breaks in the alley. And mostly they left me alone—they were too vacant to care. One day I was passing the alley and one of them asked, "You the guy that pounded Brad Dillon?"

I shrugged. I didn't even know who I'd hit—and I didn't need enemies. He took it as a yes anyway and nodded back. "That guy's an asshole."

But the main reason I liked Open Book was that on the very first day, when I climbed the stairs, I saw the girl from the library.

She was sitting by herself at a table, writing in some kind of workbook. It was a hot day, but she had on jeans and another sweater with those extra-long sleeves. I was over there before I even knew what I was doing. "Is it okay if I sit here?"

She looked at me through her glasses and then around the room. There were two teenage moms at the far end, drinking takeout coffees. There were plenty of empty tables and chairs. She looked back at her work.

I pulled out a chair. At least she hadn't said no. I sat down, and my leg started bouncing. I had to know about her name. Keeping my voice low, I said, "Hey, sorry to bother you, but you work at the library, right? Can I ask you a question?"

She kept on writing for a second and then she said, "You took money."

"What?"

"When the books fell over, you leaned across the desk and took money from the cash drawer."

"What are you talking about? I didn't take any money. From where?" If I'd learned one thing in the Bad Time, it was never cop to anything.

She didn't even blink. "I don't talk to thieves, and I don't talk to liars."

If I'd left right then, maybe I'd never have told anyone any of this. Maybe I should have left, but I couldn't. I had to know her name to know if my luck was going to run. "Look," I said, "I didn't take money from anywhere, and I'm real sorry to bother you. All I wanted was to ask your first name."

She bent over her work again. "Go away. I don't talk to liars."

Except I couldn't go away, not if I was going to keep my luck running. I sat there and said, "Well, if you saw me steal money, why didn't you tell?"

Her face got red, but she didn't look up. "Maybe I will."

"Oh, yeah? Well, if I *had* stolen money, what if I'd needed it?"

"I've heard that before."

"Well, what if I'd needed it and was never going to do it again?"

"I've heard that before too." Her head was still down, but she wasn't writing anything.

"Okay, sorry," I said. "Like I said, all I wanted to know was your first name." I pretended I was going to stand up. It didn't work. She didn't speak. I had to stand up. I started to push the chair in, saying, "I thought it was the same as somebody I used to know. Someone important to me. I thought I saw it on your name tag, but I wasn't sure."

Now she looked up. I gave her that *I wish* smile I'd given so many times to so many marks. "I'll tell you when you tell me you stole that money," she said.

I saw a way to spin it. I sat back down. "Okay. But I had to do it."

"Right."

"I did. It's this delayed-reaction condition from something bad that happened to me."

"Uh-huh."

"No, really. It was on the news and in the paper. You probably heard."

She shook her head. "I don't watch the news."

"Why not?"

"Because I was in it once too."

"Yeah, right," I said and smiled again. She didn't like that.

"I was."

"Really? What for?"

She leaned back in her chair. Her chest was as flat as her voice. "You really don't know who I am."

"I've been, uh, away," I said, "For a long time. Apart from your first name, it doesn't matter. I don't even want to know. Be anybody you want. Who do you *want* to be?"

"Who do I want to be?"

"Yeah."

For the first time, she almost smiled. "Anybody but me. Who do you want to be?"

It was a good question. I shrugged. "I don't even know who I am." I laughed to turn it into a joke. "For now my name is Danny."

"My name tag says Gillian," she said.

"Gillian?" I asked.

She said, "You say it like a *J* but spell it with a *G*."

It was close enough. My luck was running.

FIFTEEN

Maybe it was because my luck was running that I pushed it a little harder. At noon I ditched Open Book and headed back to the house. Everybody was at work or school, so I had the place to myself. I needed it.

With Harley, you'd do fakes for the day, but then you could crash. Living in RVs and motels might not seem private to you, but there were still lots of times when I'd been left alone. Here, I was Danny 24/7 and never alone. I even had to share a bedroom with Matt. The kids were always on me to do something with them. The only place I could get away from everyone was the bathroom. I'd go there and think about Meg. The walls were thin too. Once, late, I heard Roy and Shan going at it. It was too much information. After Harley and Darla had split up, if he wanted to bring someone back he would give me money for a movie, or I'd wander a mall. I was older by then. Apart from the fact that we went around robbing people blind, the wildest thing Harley would ever do was have a beer or two watching the ball game, or smoke a little weed sometimes. He didn't think I knew what it was at first, but I'd been with more that one secret smoker in the Bad Time. The point was, there was space.

Anyway, when I opened the door there was a box sitting in the hall, with a paper attached to it that said *Danny*. I guessed Carleen had stopped by with some of Danny's old stuff. There were little trophies for soccer, a Darth Vader poster, a couple of Garfield books, some lame CDs, bad drawings of motorcycles and dragons, a few photos of him and some other kids making gang signs with their hands, and one of him in his hat and shades, giving both fingers to the camera. It was crap, stupid. I left the box where it was and wondered how long I could go on doing this. I'd been Danny almost three weeks, and for now I was stuck being him. I couldn't take off until I had some cash and a plan to at least get back to the States. And even if I had those things right now, I couldn't make Danny disappear again so soon. The cops would be all over it. I'd probably barely get out of town. My best bet was still to hang in until his birthday.

And that wasn't forever, was it? My luck was running. *Do before you get done.* I made a sandwich, then did some things around the house. First, I took five dollars out of Matt's money stash in his Lego bucket. While I was at it,

I checked the cash in Shan's boot too. There was ten dollars more—even better. I took five dollars in coins. There were so many, it would be easy for Shan to think she'd miscounted. Next, I went on the computer and searched a map of Port Hope. If I was going to get out of here, it was time to get a better idea where I was. Matt had said the place was on a lake. Well, he was right—it was on Lake Ontario, a Great Lake. Danny would have called it "a big sucker." The beauty part, though, was what was on the other side: the USA. I was a boat ride from freedom.

That made me feel so good that I took Matt's bike and rode it down to the harbor. It was a *really* big lake—you couldn't see across to the other side. But there were boats there, and they looked easy to get at, and on the map the lake looked a lot longer than it was wide. Maybe the States was closer than I thought. I wondered if I could steal a boat when the time came, and how hard it was to run one. I'd never been on a boat.

I turned around and rode back to Open Book. I got upstairs just as Gillian was getting ready to leave. She didn't frown this time. "I've got something for you," I said.

"What?"

I pulled out the money I'd scored and lifted the five. "Take it back if you want."

Now she did frown.

"It's different," I said. "I made this cutting the lawn."

"Then give it back yourself," she said.

"Okay, I will. If you let me buy us coffee tomorrow. Or tea or something." She smiled a quick, tight smile and her face turned pink. She headed for the stairs. "You know I'll pay it back," I called. "See you tomorrow." It was just like snowing sales ladies in Tucson, and it was worth it. As I looked out the window and watched Gillian unlock a bike from the rack where I'd stashed Matt's, I saw Griffin, the old cop, getting into a silver Camry. Then the kid I'd jumped at school walked down the street with two other guys, maybe the ones that had been with him that day.

I waited till they were gone, then went down and got Matt's bike. Griffin was still sitting in his car, maybe waiting for somebody. He didn't look my way, so I rode on.

When I got back to Shan's, it was still early. I ditched Matt's bike at the side of the house and went in. It seemed like a good time to think about Meg.

"Who's that?" It was Roy's voice, from the living room.

"It's just me," I called. I opened and shut the refrigerator to stall for a second, getting Danny together, then I went on into the living room, making sure to toe out. Roy was in his recliner, still in his work clothes. "It's a hot sucker out there," I said.

Roy grunted. "How come you're home so early?"

I shrugged. "I got my work done, so I could go. How come you're home?"

"I put my back out at work. It hurts like hell."

"Bummer."

"Matt's bike was gone when I got home. He's not allowed to take it to school. You take it without asking?"

"No," I said. "You sure? The sucker was there just now when I came in."

He looked at me sourly. "Get me a ginger ale, will ya? It's a bugger to get up."

I got a can out of the fridge and handed it to him.

"Dude," he said, "I heard the bike hit the side of the house when you got back."

I did my confused thing, then the Danny smirk. "I bumped into it. So what?"

Roy shook his head. "You really haven't changed, have you? Shoplifting, getting kicked out of school…Listen, *Danny*"—he bit down hard on the name—"don't take things that don't belong to you without permission. Got it? That's the second damn bike I've had to buy for Matt. And don't make things hard for Shan either, 'specially by lying. She's got enough problems with your mom and that dickwad Ty. You don't like it here, see how you like it at Carleen's—and I don't care what your social worker says."

"Sure, Roy. Okay." I nodded and bounced and Danny-smiled. Then I promised myself I'd flush his dope down the toilet before I left.

SIXTEEN

At dinner that night, Roy, who was propped up with cushions, said he thought I should get a part-time job so I'd "learn responsibility" and wouldn't have so much time on my hands. I said that sounded good to me. I'd never had a straight job, and maybe Danny never had either, but I figured I could hack it, and I needed the money. Shan called a friend and arranged for me to start work for Dave the Garden Fairy that Saturday.

Thursday and Friday, I went to Open Book. Partly I had to—well, I had to leave the house, anyway, because Roy was home with his sore back. Mainly, though, I wanted to guarantee my good luck, whatever it cost.

Gillian was there ahead of me both days. I sat down beside her on Thursday morning. Right away, without even looking up, she said, "Did you take the money back?"

"Soon as the library opens," I said. At ten o'clock I walked over to the library, signed out a book and, when the clerk turned away, dropped the five-dollar bill on the floor behind the counter. I hung around by the doors until I saw her notice the money and pick it up, then went back to Gillian. "Done," I said, sitting back down. "Go ask them if they found five dollars, if you don't believe me. When do you want to go for coffee or something?" At lunchtime she let me buy her tea.

Friday, she insisted on buying *me* something, which was good because I was out of money and didn't want to take anymore right away. I was hoping the Garden Fairy would pay me Saturday, the same day I worked. Gillian said she was just going to be at Open Book until she and her mom and sister moved.

"When's that?" I didn't want to lose my luck.

She shrugged. "Whenever we sell the house."

I didn't like that. How long did it take to sell a house? It helped keep me at Open Book all day, as if I had to soak up as much luck as I could while it was still there. I even did some work to pass the time. I told the teacher I wanted to start with English, so I spent the time reading *To Kill a Mockingbird*, which I'd already read, and then answering lame questions in a workbook and listening to the babies cry. There are worse ways to spend a day.

I got the Garden Fairy joke when Dave pulled up on Saturday morning. He was a bulldog of a guy with a laugh like a chainsaw revving. Two fingers on his left hand were just stubs. "I had an argument with a lawn mower once," he said as he showed me how to start one up. "I lost."

Dave drove around in a bright yellow pickup with *Garden Fairy* painted on the sides. We went to three different places that first day, cutting lawns and trimming hedges and bushes. Shan had packed me a lunch. Dave loaned me gloves, but I still got blisters. It was hard work, but I didn't mind much. It felt good to be outside, doing stuff, and I didn't have to do much Danny. The only time I thought about him was when Griffin drove by once.

The best part of the day was at the very end. By then it was cool and looking like rain. Dave the Garden Fairy and I drove a load of cuttings to a place just outside of town where he knew he could dump them. You could see the lake in the distance. We bumped down a dirt path that followed a creek along the side of a field and suddenly came out on an embankment above the lake shore. I helped Dave pitch the grass and leaves into a gully. Dave stopped for a smoke. His gray Notre Dame T-shirt had big patches of sweat. I felt pretty grubby myself.

"Okay if I go down on the beach?" I asked.

"Be my guest." Dave waved his hand. Even with fingers missing, it was the size of a pot roast. I scrambled down. Barely a mile from town, it looked as if you were in the wilderness. The lake was like an ocean. Waves were rolling, and they were loud, too, like white noise from a TV not hooked up to cable. I threw stones into the water, but my arms were already sore from working, so I sat down on a log until Dave finished his cigarette, imagining what it would be like on the other side.

When Dave dropped me at Shan's, he paid me fifty dollars cash, Canadian. I liked that. It sounds weird, but it was the most cash I'd ever had that was truly mine. Harley might give me cash for the movies or for snacks, but he'd handled everything else. One time I'd asked him how come I didn't get more, and he said, "Room and board. And your college fund." A few days later he gave me an iPod and let me stock it up on iTunes. He said a kid like me would carry one. Mostly, though, it was for show. Harley had never let me use it when we were working or when he wanted me to play his memory games as we drove. I wondered where it was now, and whether you could use Canadian money in the States.

Sunday, I was stiff as a board and my hands were sore. It didn't matter. I had money in my dresser drawer. Shan was happy I'd done okay with Dave. Even Roy wasn't bitching at me, maybe because his back felt better. That afternoon I asked to borrow Matt's bike (he was playing a video game) and rode back out to where we'd dumped the leaves. The lake was calmer and the sun was out. You could feel heat coming up off the sand and stones. I sat on the stones with my back against a log for a while and listened to the waves lapping, and I felt myself relax. It felt good. It felt like the first time in forever.

After a while I explored a little. A few yards up the beach were the ashes of an old campfire, with some blackened beer tins mixed in. In the weeds was a rusted cogwheel that looked as if it could have been from some ancient tractor or mad scientist's machine, and on the pebbles was an old running shoe with dried seaweed clotted on the laces. I dragged some driftwood over to the log and made a little shelter. I balanced the cogwheel on one end of the log and hung the running shoe off one branch of the driftwood. There was even a block of washed-up Styrofoam to use for a seat. I hung out there for a while and looked at little boats far out on the water and felt like Robinson Crusoe. When I went back to Shan's I felt calmer than I had in a long time. Having an edge is good, but I didn't mind calmer at all.

Monday, I hit Open Book early, even before Gillian, and she came to sit with me when she got there. That made me feel even better. At lunch, she came out with me to the coffee shop on the corner.

"What happened to your hands?" she asked.

"I worked all Saturday. Made fifty bucks." I told her about Dave the Garden Fairy. "It was a little harder than I'm used to."

"Dave's nice," she said. "He used to work at our house." She looked out the window.

I didn't ask why Dave didn't work there anymore. Instead, I told her about going down on the beach the first time, and how nice it was being there by myself for a few minutes. I didn't tell her about going back though. That was private. All she said was, "It's nice being alone."

"Yeah," I said. "Where Danny was, like, you could never be alone."

She nodded. "I've felt like that. It's a drag." She looked out the window again. "How come you said *Danny*, as if he's someone different from you?"

"It just—it helps keep stuff away. Sometimes I don't want to be him. Anymore."

She looked at me. She stood up. "We should go back. I want to finish my work."

"What for?" I said.

"So things won't be even more messed up when I start at a new school."

I followed her out of the coffee shop. What I'd said wasn't exactly a lie. I didn't want to feel like Danny, or me, for that matter, when I was around Gillian. That was the main part, and it was completely true. But I know the way I said it wasn't exactly the truth. It wasn't what she meant. Did I want her to know I wasn't Danny? I don't know what I wanted—it just came out. I was sort of telling lies to tell the truth. Weird, I know, but what can I say? It felt right. That's all I can say.

SEVENTEEN

That week was good. Roy felt better and went back to work. Dave the Garden Fairy called and asked me to work again. I went to the library once and to the beach once. Carleen stayed away. Shan tied herself up in knots explaining that Carleen and Tyson got distant sometimes and that she knew Carleen was still feeling guilty about what went on with us before. Let her, I thought. Who knew what it might get me? All in all, everyone else was happy as clams, as Harley used to say. I began to think Danny and I might have just enough in common to make this a good gig.

At supper one night Shan smiled and said, "I hear you've made a friend. Fran at the clinic—no, Brooklynne, you don't need more ketchup—Fran told me she saw you having lunch with Gillian Dewitt."

I was going to say no, as usual, but I felt my face get hot.

"It's a small town, hon. Just like always."

"It was just lunch," I said.

"Gotta start somewhere." That was Roy.

"Danny gots a girlfriend," said Brooklynne.

"I didn't even know her last name," I said. I shoved a chicken finger in my mouth. It was those and mac and cheese for dinner.

"Who's Gillian Dewitt?" Matt asked.

"Duh," Shan said. "Her sister Janelle's in your class. They used to come in to the eye clinic when I was on reception there. She's a nice girl. I heard she took it pretty hard, about her dad and all."

I almost didn't want to know. It didn't seem fair, since I didn't want to tell Gillian about my past either. Roy said, "What about him?"

"Oh, you remember," Shan said. "Last year. He was the one ran that investing service, stole all those people's money and ran off."

"Riiiight." Roy slathered margarine on Wonderbread. "Couple older guys at work got burned in that." He did his big-guy chuckle. "Better not tell her how much you make with Dave there, Danny." Roy inhaled half the bread slice. "Speaking of money," he said with his mouth full, "maybe you should talk to some of those reporters and TV people." He swallowed. "Maybe we could turn your story into some real money."

Shan glared at him and shifted in her seat.

"Ow," said Roy. "What're you kickin' me for? I'm just saying—"

"He's been through enough. We don't want reporters and all that coming around, all over us."

"Geez, it's not like it'd be some, whatsit, *60 Minutes* scandal thing. He'd be a hero."

"No," I said.

"No," said Shan. "He's just a kid. Look what happened at school already."

"Fine." Roy scowled. "I'm just sayin'. I bet they'd pay a nice price for an interview. Your loss." He shot me a look. "And ours. It's not like it costs nothing for you to live here."

I gave him the Danny smirk. I wanted to take the macaroni and shove it in his face. Maybe I should have. It would have been almost the last good thing that happened for a long time.

The next day, Gillian and I took our lunches to the park across from the library. It still felt a lot like summer. Wasps kept straying over from the trash bin. We were sitting side by side at a picnic table, with our legs stretched out and our backs leaning against the table edge. Gillian was taller than me.

"I have to work at the library after school," she said. Like always, she was wearing jeans, this time with a yellow long-sleeved top. It made her arms look long and thin.

Her fingers were long and thin too. She had green-and-white-striped laces in her running shoes. "What are you doing?"

"I have to work with Dave the Garden Fairy tomorrow."

On her lap she had a zippered, blue, padded lunch box. I'd had one like it once, back in the Bad Time. She didn't unzip it. She gazed at the library. "I mean, what are you doing today?"

I shrugged. "Going back out to the beach, maybe. I made this little place to sit. It's great. All quiet, and nobody goes there." It seemed okay to tell her. Now that I knew her dad was gone, I felt as if we were tighter than ever.

"Is it out by the railway tracks? Down a path across the field?"

"Yeah." I was surprised. "You know it?"

"I've never been there, but kids go down there to party sometimes."

"Oh. Yeah. I saw a campfire and some beer cans, but nobody's been there in a long time. It's pretty private. You could come with me sometime." All at once I wanted her luck for there, too. I waved away a wasp. She still hadn't said anything. I looked at her. She was blushing. "What?" I said.

Then I got it. She thought—My own face got hot. I spoke fast. "Listen, like, I didn't...I mean, I don't...like, I can't—" And then I realized what *that* sounded like.

It was the first time I'd lost it with words since I was little. Finally I said, looking away and swatting at a wasp that wasn't even there, "I mean, I *can*, but I didn't mean… about you." I heard my voice melting away until it was barely a whisper. "I just…I don't like touching, because of some things people did to me."

I wished I was a car fading down the highway. I must have been the color of a taillight. I didn't even know why I was saying all that. I'd never spent time with girls. I'd never done anything with them either. Harley used to tease me sometimes. He'd say, "I'll buy you a piece for sweet sixteen. That kind of touching you'll like." Then he'd grin and pop his gum. I'd never known whether he was joking. Now I never would.

Gillian still didn't unzip her lunch box. Her fingers rested on top of the padded blue box. I didn't want to look up any higher. She said, "I asked what you were doing because I'm going to the movie at the mall tonight with my sister and I wanted someone to go with me. But it's okay if you can't."

I looked at her. She was still looking away, her cheeks only pink now. "Really? I mean, yeah, sure I can." It was like a date, kind of. I mean, I guessed it was. Danny was going on a date. *I* was going on a date. How weird was that? Then I had my first going-on-a-date thought: the mall was over in Cobourg, the next town. "How will we get there?"

"My mom can drive," Gillian said, "and pick us up after." She smiled. Then she stopped. She was looking at a car parked in front of the library. It was a silver Camry. "What does he want?" Gillian said. As if he was answering her, Griffin waved me over.

EIGHTEEN

"I'll be right back," I said to Gillian.

I put down my lunch and headed toward him, toeing out. I could feel myself still grinning from talking to Gillian. I crossed the street and stood at the driver's-side window. It was down, Griffin's arm still hanging out from when he'd waved me over. He looked more like cement than ever, his big gut in a gray sweatshirt spilling over faded jeans. Even the car seats were gray. "Sorry to interrupt," he said. He didn't sound it.

"S'okay. It's my lunch hour." I gave him the smirk—full-on Danny.

"How's school?"

"Good."

"Rough start, I hear."

I shrugged and smirked some more.

"Gillian's a nice girl. Meet her at Open Book?"

"Yeah."

He looked past me, toward her. "Too bad about her dad. Ruined a lot of people. Old folks mostly, on pensions. Some of them lost their homes." He tapped the door with his thumb. "I lost a little myself." Then he made a little snort, a cop laugh. "He was a helluva liar." He looked back at me. "Fooled everybody. Including me."

"That's too bad."

"It is too bad. Anyway, that's not why I'm here. Got something for you." He reached into the back and handed me a paper. It was a photocopy of two head-and-shoulders pictures, taken from the front and the side, of a guy with the numbers 61472 in front of him. Mug shots. The guy was young and thin, with a mullet, bad skin and a shoe-salesman moustache.

My heart started pounding in my ears. "Who's this sucker?" I already knew who it was.

"Michael Bennett Davidson," Griffin said. "Also known as Michael Bennett, David Bennett, Bennett Michaels, Ben Michaelson, Michael Norton, Harley Bennett, David Benson…the list goes on. You'd know him as the guy who got you to Tucson. What did he want you to call him?"

Harley, I thought, finally getting it—Harley-Davidson. "Mike," I said. "Just Mike." I wondered if Bill Blessing was on the list somewhere. I hoped not. "Like, who was he?" I had to ask, but I wanted the pounding in my ears to shut out the answer.

Griffin sighed, hoisted his eyebrows and rhymed it off. "Out of Dayton, Ohio. Did short time for fraud and possession of stolen in Illinois and Minnesota in the early nineties, arrests in San Francisco and Portland, Oregon, after that. He might have lived in Portland for a while in the mid- to late nineties, but mostly it looks as if he kept on the move. Known to police, as they say, here and there. Age at death, forty-two."

I looked again at the mug shots. Young Harley looked back at me. Griffin said something I missed. I looked up.

"How long were you with him, do you think?" he said again.

I shrugged. "I dunno. A few weeks, maybe a month."

Griffin nodded. "Remember places you went?"

"Not really. It wasn't exactly my territory. I kept asking if we were going north yet, and he'd say to leave the driving to him."

Another nod. "He ever try anything on you?"

I shook my head.

"I ask because he seems to have had a history of traveling around with young boys, claiming they were his sons. He was with one two years ago in Maryland, and another last winter in Florida."

I felt a little dizzy. I put one hand on the car roof.

"Or maybe it was the same boy." He did a slow, owl-style blink. "Who knows? The question then would be, what happened to them? You might have got off very lucky indeed, especially after that first van you climbed into."

"Maybe," I said. I was sweating. "Maybe I deserved a break." I needed one now. This guy knew too much.

"Maybe you did." Griffin paused and shifted in his seat. The car bobbed under my hand. "How's the family? Shannon okay?"

"Yeah. She's glad I'm home."

"I know she is. She deserves some happy. How about Carleen? Hugs and kisses?"

"She's okay."

"Yeah, I heard you went shopping together. How's Ty?"

"Haven't seen him. His car got repo'd."

"Lucky you. Back in the day, some people thought, given those two, you might have just taken off."

I squeezed out, "It happened likc I said." *Never change your story.*

He nodded again. "I thought different."

"Aren't you retired?" I said. It was casy to sound angry. "You don't have to think anymore. Shouldn't you be playing golf or something?"

"I hate golf," he said. "Swofford plays golf. You know what golf is? 'A good walk spoiled.' You know who said that?"

I shook my head.

"Mark Twain. Know him?"

I nodded.

"I thought you would. They tell me you're a reader now. That's nice."

"Who tells you that?"

"Lots of people tell me things." Griffin reached into the back again and came up with a paperback. "Here. This is for you too."

He held it out to me. I looked at it but didn't take it. *The Adventures of Huckleberry Finn,* by Mark Twain. Two scraps of paper stuck out from the page tops. "I already read it," I said—and I had, a long time ago.

"Try it again," said Griffin. "I marked a couple of places you'll enjoy."

I took it. I figured it was better to see what was on his mind.

He started his car. "Stay safe."

"You better put your seat belt on," I said. "You don't want to break the law."

I watched him until he pulled away. By then I thought I could move without trembling. I folded the copy of Harley's pictures into the book and waded back to Gillian through a wave of Bad Time. "What time is the movie?" I asked.

NINETEEN

I wanted to take off for the beach right then and just think it all through, but everything went wrong. Mr. Hunter at Open Book wanted to talk about my "learning plan." When I got back to Shan's, Roy made me and Matt wash his pickup truck, because his back was hurting. Then Shan wanted me to help with dinner. While I was spreading fish sticks and frozen fries on a baking sheet, she asked me to take Matt to the movies after supper because Brooklynne was at a birthday-party sleepover and she and Roy wanted a little "down time." I knew what that meant. When I told her I was already going to a movie with Gillian and her sister, she said, "That's perfect! Janelle's in Matt's class. Ma-att!" and then it was done. What could I say?

The Dewitts picked us up at eight in a white Jeep Liberty that smelled like dog inside. Gillian's mom had sharp eyes in a soft, tired face. She wore pricey-looking preppy clothes—tan jacket, designer jeans, boat shoes— and her long coppery hair was held back with a velvet headband. I sat in front with her. She was a fast driver, and she talked a lot about not much, which was fine with me. I gave her my nice-boy-in-the-shopping-mall routine. The only time we got close to saying anything real was when she said, "It must be nice for you to be home."

"Yes, ma'am, and a little strange too." I knew she must have heard my story. I guessed that meant Gillian knew some of it now too. In the back, the little sister, Janelle, was yakking away. Gillian was quiet, and Matt seemed to be tongue-tied.

The movie was at the same mall as the store where I'd boosted the clothes. When Roy wasn't looking, Shan had given me money for me and Matt, which was good. I'd forgotten how expensive movies and snacks are. If I'd had to do it on my Garden Fairy money, I would have been screwed.

Janelle got Matt talking after a bit. Gillian and I didn't talk much. It was better in the theater, where I could sit beside her and just be there. I didn't want to say, "Your mom knows about me," so I just said, "It's been a long time since Danny's been at a movie." *I'd* been to one about a week before Harley died.

Gillian smirked. "Did he go to the beach today?"

"He didn't have time," I said. "But I'll go for him tomorrow." I didn't say it, but her joking like that made me like her a lot. I wasn't going to ask about her. She wasn't going to ask about me. We were just going to be whoever we were right now.

After the show, we had to wait for Mrs. Dewitt to pick us up. "Everything's closed," Janelle complained.

"Green Leaf isn't," Matt said. He turned to me. "Let's see if Grandma is working. Last time, she gave us free candy."

"Huh?" I hadn't known the store where Carleen worked was in the same mall. The last thing I wanted was for Gillian to see me with her. A week ago, I would have figured it would get me more sympathy. Now it was different. Not that it mattered. Matt had already started toward Green Leaf, and Janelle was right behind him. I shrugged at Gillian and we followed.

It was ten thirty. The grocery was at the far end of the mall. It was open, but it looked deserted. There was one cashier in a green vest at the row of checkouts and a tired-looking woman pushing a cart through the produce section. Matt and Janelle got distracted by a DVD display. Gillian stopped with them. I kept going. I figured if I went a little ahead, I could come back, say Carleen wasn't around and get us out of there.

I cut down the next aisle, glancing back to make sure they weren't following. Voices jumped out at me. I stopped just in time. A scarecrow in shapeless jeans and a faded hoodie stood with his back to me, twitching as if his wiring was faulty. "Come *on*, I come all the way down. You know how hard it was to—"

"I don't care about that. I got nothing for you. You shouldn't be here and you know it."

"I know, I know it. I wouldn't be here if I didn't have to. All I need is once."

"Are you crazy? Forget it. There's no way I—"

I knew the second voice. I was trying to back away when the scarecrow bobbed and Carleen saw me. It was a different Carleen. Her face was knotted with anger. Now her eyes flared, then her whole face wobbled, like in a bad horror movie.

"Get out of here," she hissed, flapping a hand furiously at me as if she was scatting a cat. "*Get out.*"

The scarecrow twisted around. I barely recognized him from Shan's photos. Under the hood, Tyson's face wasn't much more than a skull with a wisp of moustache and dull, crazy eyes. He looked at me blankly, arching his skinny neck as if it was stiff, his jaw wagging back and forth like a dog's tail.

Then Matt's voice floated toward us. "Hey, Danny, where—" and he barged around the corner with the rest of them. "Danny, what's goin'—"

At the second "Danny," Tyson's body arched and he stumbled back, screaming, "NO! GET...GET..." He lunged for the nearest shelf and started throwing things at us, bags of pretzels and potato chips. Janelle screamed. Carleen grabbed at him, but he shook her off. I think the rest of us were just stunned. At first I almost laughed. Then, as Carleen wrestled with him, Ty got his hand on a jar of something and heaved it. It sailed over our heads and smashed against a shelf. I ducked. Bits of glass and something wet pattered down. The smell of salsa filled the aisle. I think we all shouted then.

"Get outta here," Carleen spat, wrestling with Ty as he scrabbled for something else to throw. We ran.

TWENTY

It wasn't something you could keep secret. For one thing, we were all splattered with salsa. It was lucky none of us had been cut by the glass. It wasn't a happy ride back. Janelle spilled to her mom. Matt blurted it all out to Shan and Roy as soon as we got in the door. I didn't know what to think, except that Ty was on drugs and now I knew what Griffin meant by "stay safe."

"Oh God," Shan moaned. "He's using again. And how did he get down here?" She looked at us mournfully and started to cry. "Matt, you know Ty has a problem, right? I'm sorry you had to see this, hon. And Danny, don't take it hard. You remember, it's not him when he's like that. After you disappeared, he blamed himself. He was so, so sorry you'd fought that day. So sorry. He just tore himself apart. Said he should have gone to pick you up when you called. So now…he was just so surprised, probably, and he can't handle it when that stuff is in his system."

I nodded. "Like seeing a ghost, almost."

Her face blanched as if she'd seen one. "Oh God. Don't even—" She was in her housecoat. It had blue and yellow flowers on it. Where it fastened I could see something lacy underneath. She motioned Matt to her and gave him a hug, salsa and all. Then she tried to call the Dewitts, but their number wasn't listed. Roy just shook his head. I wondered how often he'd shaken his head after he got saddled with Shan's family. His own family lived in some faraway place called Truro. I was supposed to know where that was, but I didn't. It sounded as if the wildest thing Roy's family ever did was go bowling.

Matt and I got cleaned up. Shan let Matt stay up with me to play a video game. We killed things until we calmed down. Then I tried to sleep and shut it all out. By then, I'd forgotten all about Griffin's book.

I remembered it the next day, though, while I was working with Dave the Garden Fairy. We finished around two. I got forty dollars. Then I asked to use Matt's bike, and I rode out to the beach with *Huckleberry Finn*. I left the bike hidden in the weeds at the top of the bank and climbed down. It was breezy, and warm when the sun was out. Mountains of mashed-potato clouds drifted across the sky. The ripples on the lake had a new glare, like Danny's mirrored shades, when the sun caught them.

It made the water look cold, reminding me that it was fall. I hunkered down in my shelter, using the Styrofoam block and the log for a windbreak. It was good there. I'd lined up bits of green frosted glass like pebbles along one log and hung a cracked orange Frisbee on a stick, like a flag, beside the running shoe.

Then I opened *Huckleberry Finn*. Like I said, I'd read it before, back when it was all I'd had time to boost from a bookmobile somewhere. Fresno, maybe. I remembered thinking it was good but tough, because it was set in olden days down south. Everyone talked funny. I knew it was about Huck, who bailed on his drunk dad and rode downriver on a raft with this escaped slave, Jim. They met people and had crazy adventures before it all ended up somewhere with this other kid, Tom Sawyer. I'd liked Huck because he kept on the move and he was good at lying and faking and because once, by coincidence, I was reading it when we were riding in the van after a job and Harley merged us from a ramp onto the interstate, popped his gum and said, "We're in the river now" as we blended into the traffic. The rest was a blank.

The first slip of paper Griffin had stuck in the book was at chapter eleven. It was a part where Huck pretends to be a girl and an old lady spots that he's faking.

The second slip said *25–29*. The chapters were about Huck and two scammers showing up in a little town and pretending to be long-lost relations of a rich guy who's just died. Huck gets confused and lies his face off and then feels bad because the dead man's daughter is so nice.

I didn't read it all. I didn't have to. By now I knew what this was really all about. Griffin knew. How much didn't even matter. He was telling me he knew.

At first, the feeling wasn't even panic, just this sick sureness. I closed my eyes, then opened them, because I thought I might throw up. Another paper was sticking out of the book. I pulled out the folded sheet of mug shots. I looked at Michael Bennett Davidson. He looked back at me, just the slightest bit cocky. I could see how he'd turned into the Harley I knew. That was then. I needed him now. I needed Harley to pull up in the van and take me and Gillian away with him. But he wasn't going to, was he? In my world, no one came back, especially me.

As I folded up the mug shots and stuffed them in my pocket, the panic set in. All at once it hit me: who else knew? My brain was fast-forwarding through every talk I'd had since Shan got me on that plane. Did Carleen know? Roy? Shan? All of them? What was going on? Was I being set up for something? *Who was conning who?*

TWENTY-ONE

Maybe I'd been too long out of the Bad Time, getting soft. I scrambled up off the stones. At first, all I could think was, *Run*. I looked across the glaring lake. It hurt my eyes and there were no boats to see. I don't know why that made it worse, but it did. I grabbed the stick the Frisbee hung on and started smashing it against the log. Then I took *Huckleberry Finn* and threw it as far as I could into the lake. It wasn't very far. It floated. I heaved rocks, rocks and more rocks at it and missed every time. Then I stood there, staring at it, panting.

I had to float too. To do that, I had to chill. I'd been alone before. I'd spent my whole life alone. This was nothing compared to being a little kid in the Bad Time. It was them against me again. If I could get out of Josh's office, I could get out of this, whatever *this* was.

I took a big, shaky breath and picked up what was left of the stick. It was bent in the middle. I tried to straighten it. The pieces almost fit back together, but it was still bent. Unless they were all Oscar-winning actors, the family believed me. Gram and Grampy, Uncle Pete…all of them. Nobody was asking questions. I figured Carleen and Ty were too wasted to know better. Shan had said Carleen was sober, but anyone could tell that hadn't lasted. And Shan…Shan…Was I wrong about her? Needles of doubt came back to prick me. But why would she do all this if she knew? It made no sense. Did it? I threw the stick away.

Okay then, what did Griffin know? What could he know? What could anybody know? Danny had been gone three years. There were no fingerprints to check. There was DNA, but Shan had joked that my DNA was the same. Why would she do that if she didn't believe me? They couldn't check mine if we didn't agree to it. Would she say no if Griffin asked her for a DNA sample? I could tell she didn't like him.

By this time, I was tromping circles on the beach. If Griffin had proof, he'd just have me arrested me, right? If he didn't, he couldn't do anything unless I blew it. Maybe he was jerking my chain, trying to make me run and give myself away. He'd said people thought Danny ran off. Shan had almost said the same thing on the plane. What was that about?

The waves had almost brought *Huckleberry Finn* back to shore. I kicked at it and got soaked. The last part of those chapters, the part I hadn't read, I remembered. Huck and the con men get caught when what look like real relatives show up. Did Griffin know where Danny was? Was the real Danny going to show up? Was he telling me to run before it was too late? *Why?* Why, why, why? I thought I'd calmed down, but now I had to move again. I had to get out of there.

I was starting up the bank when they came over its crest. For half a beat I didn't recognize them; I hadn't seen them since my first day at Open Book, when I spotted them from the window. The guys from the high school hallway. One was lugging a grocery bag that looked to be stuffed with beers, another had newspaper—to start a beach fire, I guessed. The one I'd jumped was lighting a cigarette or a joint. Now we were face to face, maybe ten feet apart, and it was all downhill for them. "It's him," one of them shouted. Smoker Boy—Dillon or whatever his name was— looked up, startled.

I'll tell you a good reason not to smoke: you have a better chance of outrunning a smoker who wants to kick the crap out of you. I took off along the beach toward town, the beach stones sliding and crunching crazily under my feet. I could hear him—or maybe them— behind me, swearing, their steps out of time with mine. It felt like forever. Then their noise fell back and something whirred past my head. A rock smacked into the clay bank, then another. One smashed into my left shoulder, and pain rocketed down my arm. I stumbled and went down over a piece of driftwood. My head banged something, my knee something else, but I kept rolling forward and then was back up again, gasping, running. I kept on running, around a bend in the shore and until I was far out of range and couldn't run anymore.

My breath tore at my throat. My head and shoulder were throbbing, and I could feel stinging on my forehead. It was bloody when I touched it, and a big goose egg was coming up. At least I could move my arm. My new jeans were torn at one knee, and I could feel more stinging there. I limped along the rest of the beach to town and came out in a tired little playground by the harbor. At first it felt deserted.

A dog barked. A voice I knew called, "Buster!"

I looked up and there was Gillian.

TWENTY-TWO

S he had one of those retractable leashes and a plastic bag. She clipped the leash back on Buster's collar and he calmed down, sniffing me as I stood there aching. "Are you all right? What happened? Did your brother—"

"Not Danny's brother. I had an accident."

"On the beach?"

I closed my eyes. "Remember the place I like? You said kids went there to party. Those guys I had trouble with showed up while I was there."

"Oh God. Did you have a fight?"

The yes was almost out of my mouth. I looked at her. "I ran. They got me with a rock." I looked away, across the lake. "Sometimes," I said, "I just want to go to the other side."

"It's not very exciting," Gillian said.

"You've been?" For a second, I didn't hurt. "How'd you get there?"

She shrugged. "Well, our boat. I went across one time with…" Her voice trailed off. I should have paid more attention, but I was too excited.

"Your boat? Do you have a boat? Where is it?" I had a crazy picture of the two of us just taking off.

"It's over there." She tilted her head. I looked and saw Mrs. Dewitt talking to a man in a pickup truck. Behind the truck was a big boat trailer with a cabin cruiser on it. "Only it's not ours anymore," Gillian finished.

"Oh."

"The season's over anyway. That's why everyone's taken their boats out."

I looked again. She was right, of course. No wonder the place looked deserted.

"Anyway, it wasn't so great. It rolls more out there. I got sick. And Oak Orchard isn't exactly exciting."

"Well," I said, "at least it's not far."

She squinted behind her glasses. "It took us all day."

"Oh," I said again. "Where Danny used to live, it was less." I didn't know if that was right. It didn't matter. The main thing was, escaping across the lake was a goner. Everything started to hurt. The sun had gone behind those mashed-potato clouds. It was chilly. "I should probably go." I limped a step. I'd stiffened up standing there.

"Do you want a ride?" Gillian asked.

That's when I remembered. I swore. "I left Matt's bike behind."

"Where?"

"I hid it in the long grass on top of the bank."

"Come on," Gillian said. "My mom can drive us."

I limped over to the Jeep with her and we waited until her mom had finished talking to the guy taking the boat. "That's another job done," she said as she joined us. She didn't look any too pleased to see me. Then again, why would she after I'd gotten a jar of salsa thrown at her kids' heads?

I sucked it up and did my best with the sympathy card. "I'm real sorry about last night, Mrs. Dewitt. Shan tried to call but couldn't get your number. You know I've been, uh, away a long time, and I didn't know anything about Ty."

Then Gillian said I'd had an accident and asked her mom to drive us to the bike. I rode in the back with Buster. Gillian said he was a golden Lab. I understood now why the Jeep smelled like dog. It made me sneeze, which didn't make my shoulder feel any better.

I asked Mrs. Dewitt to let me out at the top of the dirt track. "It's kind of muddy down there. You don't want to get stuck."

"I'll come with you." Gillian got out too. I shook my head. She ignored me.

The bike was a couple hundred yards down the trail. You could smell wood smoke and weed in the breeze as we got closer. The bike was lying deep in the tall grass where I'd left it. I peeked over the bank. They were sitting in my spot, with a little fire going and a line of beer tins already on one of the logs, their voices mixing with the sound of the water. I wanted to roll a boulder onto them. But there weren't any boulders, and I had bigger problems. I got the bike and we started up the road.

When we were well away, I said, "I am sorry about last night. Danny has a weird family."

"That's okay," Gillian said. "So do I."

We were on either side of the bike. She smiled. That made me feel good. She tucked her hair behind her ears. She looked, well, pretty. I wanted to say it, but it was hard. I could say a million nice things I didn't mean, but saying one I did was harder than catching Harley dealing off the bottom of the deck. I did it though. Gillian smiled and looked even prettier.

"Thank you."

"Maybe we could go to another movie," I said. "Just us."

"Us?" she teased. "Does Danny want to go to another movie?"

"I don't know about Danny, but I do."

"Me too."

For a minute I forgot all about Griffin and Tyson. I even forgot to hurt. Gillian helped me put the bike in the back of the Jeep. She touched my hand, I think on purpose. I didn't mind at all.

TWENTY-THREE

For the next few days, though, I didn't think much about movies. It was a week straight from the Bad Time. Meg had found out about what happened with Ty and she was all over it, meeting with me, meeting with Carleen, knowing we all wanted to make it work. The weather was cooler now. She wore clingy sweaters. They weren't as nice as tops I could look down.

I could feel myself slipping back into my old Bad Time ways, too. I stopped talking. I looked away from everyone. I got stupid. One night after supper, Brooklynne kept pestering me to play with her doll stuff until I tipped the dollhouse over and said it was an accident. She started crying, of course, and everyone, especially Roy, was pissed off.

After that I took Matt's bike without asking and just rode. I ended up out at the beach again. I shouldn't have gone back; they'd wrecked it all, of course. It was windy and empty and the waves were pounding. Why I'd ever thought I could get across the lake I didn't know. I stood there and yelled into the wind, not even words, just noise, and it was as if I wasn't even yelling at all. I went back to the bike. It had a flat tire. By the time I walked back to town, it was after dinner. Shan was in tears, thinking I might have gone again. Matt was freaking about his bike being stolen. Brooklynne was running around yelling, and Roy was pissed all over again.

I lied about where I'd been. I lied about the bike. I said I'd found it down by the river where whoever stole it must have left it and I'd been lucky enough to recognize it. Meg got called all over again. *I know we all want this to work.* I'd tried not to stare at her chest.

Meanwhile, I hurt like the Bible thumpers had been beating on me, and Griffin hung over everything like a concrete nightmare. He had me second-guessing everything and everyone, including Shan. She'd say something like "You never used to like orange cheese" and instantly I'd be on guard. One time I said, "Well, sorry I can't be exactly the way you remember. Times change." She looked hurt and I felt as if I'd blown it, and I didn't know how to make it better.

Griffin had dropped out of sight. That made it worse. That told me he knew what he was doing. You worry more when you're always looking over your shoulder. Harley used to do the same thing with scams. He'd set the bait and then pull back for a few days, playing hard to get. The marks would drown in their own greed. "It's not outta sight, outta mind," he'd say. "It's outta sight, *in* the mind." I was learning the hard way that he was right. Knowing Griffin's mind game didn't keep it from working.

He had me aching to run. I had to get ready. The only place I could think of to go to was Reno. When Darla and Harley split a couple years back, Darla headed there. She said she was tired of the road and had connections at a casino there. I thought if I could find her, maybe she could help me a little. Darla didn't owe me anything, but she'd been okay to me, and she knew I did good work. She was also pretty much the only other person I really knew.

To get to Reno, I'd have to get across the border and have money for food and bus fare plus a little padding. Toronto was a pretty big city not too far from Port Hope. I'd start by going there. On the map, it looked as if I could go from Toronto to Niagara Falls. I was sure I could cross the border there. I had a backpack, clothes, ID. I wondered if I could steal more ID from someone at Open Book. I also needed to work out the longest head start I could get and round up as much cash as I could.

First chance I got, I looked for Darla on Facebook on a library computer. She'd used a couple different last names. No luck. Then I checked Matt's and Shan's money stashes and got the next bad news: the money was gone. When I cornered him, Matt told me that Roy had opened a savings account for him. Then Shan came home from shopping with a bunch of new clothes, so I knew where hers had gone, and Roy hit me up for twenty-five dollars for my share of a birthday gift for her. I was down to forty dollars Canadian, all I had left from working with Dave the Garden Fairy. I wasn't going to get far with that.

I did the only thing I could think of. I'd remembered a kind of Hail Mary play Harley had told me how to run if you were going to take off instantly and needed cash, but you needed a bank card for it. I went to the bank and opened an account with twenty-five of the forty dollars. Getting my card would take a few days, they said. Till then, at least most of my cash was hidden away from tightwad Roy—I could see him going through *my* dresser drawer.

In the meantime, my only chance for a quick score looked to be a family party for Shan on the weekend. With any luck, Gram and Grampy might slip me a few bucks, or I could sneak a look through some purses. I asked if Gillian could come to the birthday party with me. I told myself it was good cover for Danny, and it was. With someone else there, it would be okay if I acted a little differently. But really, I just wanted her there. Luckily, she said yes.

Gillian helped me pick a birthday card for Shan. Roy had told me to get a card we could all give to her. When I used to have time to kill in malls while Harley was busy, I'd sometimes looked at birthday cards, deciding which ones I'd have liked to get. I'd never picked one for some-body else.

"How old is she going to be?" Gillian asked as we stood at the display.

I didn't have a clue. "Thirty-two," I said.

"So it's not, like, a significant birthday."

"I guess not."

"How about that one?" It had a picture of a goldfish in sunglasses and some kind of lame joke about hoping the birthday "makes a splash."

"Sure," I said. "When's your birthday?"

"In February." She passed me the card. "Which one would you pick for yourself?"

She laughed. "I don't know. You can't do that—it wouldn't be a surprise."

"It's just a game I play," I said.

"Well, then, which one would you pick?" She'd turned it around on me.

"That one." The card had a cartoon of four fat butts, jeans sagging off them. Inside it said, *The backside of Mount Rushmore. Have a monumental birthday,* and there was a cartoon of the four faces on the mountain.

"That's what I would have picked too."

"Get out." I laughed. "You would not."

"Okay, that one." It was a perky cartoon face exclaiming, *You're cheerful, kind, talented, funny, smart, generous, friendly, helpful, sympathetic, hardworking, passionate, creative...* Inside it finished with...*and you'll believe anything. Believe this: Happy Birthday!* "When's *your* birthday?" she asked.

It was a good question. Danny's was in November, so that was what I had to say. I'd have to check the birth certificate back at Shan's for the date. I was getting sloppy. The thing was, I didn't want to tell Gillian *Danny's* birthday. I wanted to tell her mine—except I wasn't sure when it was either. There were a lot of years in the Bad Time when no one bothered to ask, and if anyone did, I always said it was the month before— I wasn't going to tell anyone I'd forgotten. When I was with Harley and Darla, Darla asked me one time. We were up in Washington State. It was raining. We'd scored big all week.

"Whaddya mean, last month?" Harley had demanded. It was hard to lie to Harley. He could practically always tell, maybe because he was such a good liar himself. "I bet he's just saying that. Whaddya think, Dar? I bet he's just scared we'll give him the paddywhacks."

"Could be." Darla half smiled, reaching for her smokes.

Harley said, "All right, he won't tell, so we get to pick one. How about today?"

"Today?" I said. I didn't like being teased. I didn't like paddywhacks either.

"Why not? What's today? Check the paper."

I remember it was a Spokane paper. I picked it up off the RV seat. "March twenty-ninth."

"Bingo. That's your birthday. Remember it." *Pop* went Harley's gum. That night we had pizza in a restaurant and the waiters sang "Happy Birthday" and Harley and Darla let me spend twenty bucks in Barnes & Noble. I got a book of Sherlock Holmes stories. I put the steak knife under my mattress again, just in case they remembered the paddywhacks.

I had to answer Gillian's question, so I said, "Not until late spring."

When I left her that afternoon, I went back to the store and bought the card she'd liked. Neither of us was going to be here in February.

TWENTY-FOUR

The birthday party for Shan was up at Uncle Pete's place, in the country north of town. We picked Gillian up in the family van. The Dewitt house was classy and old-looking, on the steep hill of a street where even the doghouses were probably mansions. There was a FOR SALE sign staked into the front lawn. It was pretty clear that the Garden Fairy hadn't flown by in a while.

You could tell Shan was pleased I'd invited Gillian. She made a fuss over her, asking after her mom and sister. Gillian wore a red hoodie over her jeans, and she had a jacket with her. Uncle Pete had promised a bonfire after dinner.

Uncle Pete's place was a summer cabin—a cottage, they called them up there—that he'd added on to and converted into a house. It was by a lake the size I wished

Lake Ontario was. I knew from some of the home movies I'd watched that Danny had gone there a lot. Pretending to be forgetful was only going to take me so far. I asked Pete first thing what had changed since I'd been away, and he took Gillian and me on a tour. He said he'd taken the dock in for the season and that his boat was in storage, and I came up with a couple "memories" of fishing that I'd watched at Shan's. Then he showed us how he'd redone the kitchen and put in a new bathroom "that you won't remember." He was right. I said it was good to be back.

Uncle Pete's grown kids were there too, with their own kids. After supper we all took lawn chairs down to the fire pit by the water and Uncle Pete got the bonfire going. The dark came on as Matt and Brooklynne and Uncle Pete's grandkids ran around with hissing sparklers. Gram and Grampy were blathering about getting ready to head to Florida. I sat next to Gillian, sunk in one of those saggy fold-up chairs that have beer-can holders in their arms. The heat from the fire was on my face and the night air was at my back. Uncle Pete passed out sticks for toasting marshmallows. From the joking, I got the picture that Danny had been some kind of marshmallow-toasting fanatic, which didn't make me happy. I don't much like marshmallows for one, and I haven't been crazy about getting close to fire ever since Wayne the Bible thumper held my hand over the stove element. You better believe I wasn't getting near those sparklers.

"C'mon, Danny," Gillian said. She was already crouching, reaching into the heat. The light from the fire made her seem to glow too. I was about to say I had to use the washroom first and then slip back to the house to hit the purses when I noticed something. The sleeve of her hoodie had pulled up, and in the firelight two pale ridges on the underside of her wrist were showing. They gave me kind of a jolt. I knew what they were. I'd met kids in the Bad Time who'd done that to themselves. She had just turned to look at me, probably wondering why I hadn't said anything, when headlights swept the lawn and a car with a bad muffler pulled in. We all turned.

"Better late than never," said Uncle Pete. The motor cut out. There was a splash of light from inside the car. Two people. The doors clunked and they came toward us, surrounded by kids' sparklers: Carleen and Ty.

All at once Shan was beside me. "I didn't know if they were coming or not, hon."

I looked at her. Gillian stood up, and Shan touched her arm. "He's really sorry for what happened. He slipped, he knows, and he wants to apologize. And Gillian, I wouldn't have let you come, hon, if I didn't know it would be one hundred percent okay. Our Ty's had some issues, and I'm so sorry you had to be involved. If you'd been hurt I'd never have forgiven myself and neither would Ty. But this—this is just going to be fun. It's my birthday!"

Gillian looked kind of worried. I probably looked the same way.

"C'mon, you two," Shan coaxed. "He won't be in your face. He's shy. Just let him take his time and you'll see."

Roy had come up behind her. His eyes caught mine and rolled. It might have been the one time we felt the same about something. He'd calmed down after I'd gotten the card and given him an extra ten bucks for Shan's gift.

Carleen was in jeans and a Dale Earnhardt NASCAR jacket. Her face was a hatchet, sharp and dangerous in the firelight. Tyson was a step or two behind her. This time he had on a ballcap and a jean jacket over a hoodie, and he was carrying a can of beer. People called out hellos and he lifted the can like a toast. "Yo."

"Sorry we're late," Carleen said, then to Shan: "Happy birthday, dreamboat."

Shan went over and kissed her. Carleen made her way around the circle until she got to Gillian and me. Gillian's sleeve was back over her wrist.

"Hey, Momma," I said.

Carleen looked at us. If her face was a hatchet, her eyes were razor blades. There was a hard gleam in them. "Sorry about the other night. Understand, I had to deal with Ty. He's not good with, uh, surprises." There was a little something on her breath, vodka maybe; it was hard to tell. All I could smell for sure was cigarettes. This time, with everyone watching, she went all the way and gave me something like a hug. I introduced Gillian. Carleen went through the motions. Then she turned to Tyson and jerked her head at me.

Tyson had stayed at the edge of the firelight, sipping his beer and talking to Uncle Pete. He was still bouncing and rolling but not as badly as at the grocery. Now he came over to us. I think he was trying to look casual. He looked about as casual as a funeral. "Hey-ey-ey" he said, with kind of a hoarse little chuckle breaking up his voice. "Um. Little, uh, bro, can I—can I...talk to you for a sec?"

He led me a few steps away. He turned, and the fire lit up his skeleton face. He was twitching so much now that one of the kids could have waved him around in the dark to watch the sparks fly out of his eyes. "So, uh, listen, I'm really sorry, dude. I was just so...surprised and, like, it'd been so long and...so I didn't recognize you..." The words rushed out, stumbling. He gave me the family sneer. I gave it back.

"'S all right."

"No, lissen, dude, I was outta line. Lissen, I gotta level with ya..." He fished half a joint from the top pocket of his jacket, fired it with a lighter and sucked some in. His hands shook the whole time. "You want? No? No, I gotta level with ya. It'd been so long and I'd thought, you know, even after I heard that you—like, you know I got a little problem, right?" Now the words were racing each other. He spread his hands as if I was supposed to size up a shirt he was trying on. I nodded. "Lissen, you want a beer or anything?" He yanked one out of the pouch of his hoodie.

"No, it's okay." All I wanted was for him to get done.

"Okay, so I got a problem and sometimes I don't even get things right, even when I hear them, and it had just been so long and I'd got it in my head that you were, like..."

"What?" I said. "Dead?"

"Whoo-oh, don't even *say* that, man. 'Cause you're not. You're one hundred percent alive, dude, and thank God for it." He squinted as he took another hit off the joint. "Thank God for it. But when you, uh, you know, *popped up* like that, oh man, I freaked. You know?" He blew out smoke.

"Sure."

"Anyway, uh, this is just to, just to say sorry, you know? And like I know things weren't always right between us, dude, but I—I kept somethin' of yours all the time, like a momen, monu—*memorial* of you, in case you came back. So now I wanna give it back to ya, but just between us, okay? This is just between you and me, bro to bro." He reached into another pocket, his jeans this time, and pulled something out. He took a last quick hit off the roach, threw it on the ground, grabbed my hand and pushed something into my palm. We stood there with him clamping my hand between his. "Between us, okay? No Shan, no Ma, just us. Brothers. All the way." I nodded. His eyes were like the bonfire now. He had a surprisingly strong grip, and his hands were grave-digger cold. "You may need this some time, man. I couldn't save you last time. This is for you. Never can tell. Just us? Brothers? All the way?"

He was waiting for an answer. "All the way," I said. "All the way."

And I was, too. I just didn't know it yet.

TWENTY-FIVE

"**I** saw you and Tyson had a little brother time there." Shan sounded pleased when we got home. Then she said, "He didn't want to give you drugs, did he?"

"He was smoking weed," I said. "I didn't want any."

She made a clucking sound. I didn't say he was a crackhead, crankhead, whatever he was. It didn't matter; probably we both knew that already. I said, "He apologized. Said welcome home. I think he's pretty bent up right now. Tell you the truth, I'm kind of glad he's in Peterborough."

She nodded, looking tired. "He tries, hon. I know you remember him being crazy bad before you disappeared. He should have picked you up that day. He tore himself apart about it after." Her voice was pleading. It was as if she was convincing herself as much as me.

I said, "I know. You told me. He didn't."

"I know he wanted to. He just can't always help himself. He hangs with some bad people up there, I think. Bad influences. And Momma tries to…" She bit her lip. Her shoulders began to shake. "Oh God…sometimes, this family…"

"Hey," I said. "We're here now." She gave me this huge apple-blossom smile and went to hustle Brooklynne off to bed.

Major dopers are nut cases. I'd met them before, with Harley. The "memorial" Tyson had given me was nothing special, far as I could see: a cheap gold neck chain with a letter *D* hanging from it. The clasp was broken. It was about as exciting as the other junk Carleen had brought over. I put it in some rolled-together socks at the back of my drawer. I figured I had more important things to think about.

Sunday, I checked the telephone book. There were four Griffins. I wrote down the addresses and looked them up on a town map I'd found in the kitchen junk drawer. After supper, I asked to borrow Matt's bike. Gillian had shown me how to fix the flat with a little kit she had. It was getting dark earlier now. I pedaled under streetlights.

At the second address, a silver Camry was parked in the drive. It was a good-sized, suburb-type place a block from Gillian's, on a street not as fancy. A light was on in back, in what I guessed was the kitchen. I stood under a tree, away from the streetlight, and watched until I saw Griffin. He had a plate and a glass. Blue TV light flickered on in the front room. I moved closer to the house. I don't know what I was going to do. A dog started to bark. I rode away.

TWENTY-SIX

It spooked me, seeing Griffin alone in the blue light of the TV. It was as if he had nothing to do except come after me. I had to get ready to run. I was on pins and needles until the bank card and pin number arrived the next Tuesday. "Strictly a desperation move," Harley had told me. "A one-shot before you move on, 'cause you can't go back—it burns the ID. Never tried it myself."

We'd been sitting in a coffee shop someplace down south. Atlanta, maybe. Wherever it was, it was raining and the waitress kept calling me "sugar." Harley'd spooned about five sugars of his own into his mug, and a bunch of those little cream containers too. Before energy drinks got popular, I used to watch him put sugar in Coke.

"What you do, see,"—he stopped to sip—"is you open an account with the ID, get a pin card. Then, just before you're going to split, go to a branch bank machine and key in a check deposit for whatever."

I was eating a cream-filled donut. I remember wiping cream off my chin. "What do you deposit?"

"Nothing. That's the beauty part. You just stick a piece of paper into one of the deposit envelopes, feed it in and punch in anything—five hundred, say. The machine will give you cash against it right away. If you time it right, it's at least a good eight hours before they clear the machines and find out they've been burned. By then you're long gone."

I figured five hundred would get me food and a bus to Reno and leave some for a cushion. I wouldn't work the scam until the last minute. As soon as I did, Danny wouldn't just be a runaway—he'd be wanted for theft.

Even if I had cash covered, I still needed a way to move. I was past daydreaming about crossing the lake. No buses stopped in Port Hope. There were only two trains a day, and they were both at times when everyone would notice I was gone. That left Mr. Hunter's car. His keys were always in that jacket draped over his chair at Open Book. He parked his blue Lumina behind the building. I'd done some driving with Harley, on back-roads where no one would notice.

Now that I had the bank card, the plan was simple. Pick a day, leave a note for Shan saying I was going to be late, scoop Hunter's keys, hit the bank and then the road. Hunter would still be handing out workbooks to stoners. Shan wouldn't wonder about me until I was long gone.

I figured I could make it the thirty miles to a commuter-train station, ditch the car and hop the train to Toronto, then take a night bus to the border.

Planning it was one thing. Doing it was another. I was tied up in knots. One minute I'd be sweating to get away, the next I'd decide to tough it out. I kept going past Griffin's place. It didn't help. Finally, I gave myself until Thursday. If Griffin hadn't made a move by then, I'd be gone.

There was another reason I was tied up in knots. Every time I went past Griffin's place, I went past Gillian's too. I told myself I stayed in Port Hope because she was my good luck. At Open Book now, I'd pretend to read *The Hobbit* when I was really watching her wrists, looking for those scars. She always wore tops with extra-long sleeves, though, sometimes with bracelets underneath, and she'd nip at the ends of her sleeves with her fingers as she bent over her workbook, tugging like a puppy worrying a bone. If she'd really tried to off herself because of her old man, I didn't know what to think.

It had been a long time since leaving someone had made me feel anything. I knew people were supposed to get all torn up about it, like Gillian had with her dad, but I was way past letting myself do that. You didn't do that and survive the Bad Time. Sometimes I'd have a kind of empty feeling and realize I'd been thinking about Harley, but it was easy to make sure that was as far as it got. I had enough to think about in the here and

now. And if I could keep out thoughts of Harley—and
he'd never even done anything bad to me—I could keep
out almost anything. That was the safe way.

If I could block out Harley, I could block out Gillian.
Thursday came and nothing had changed. It had to be,
then. I scooped socks and underwear from my dresser
drawer and stuck them in my pack. I had my jacket and
Danny's ID and the bank card. I left the note for Shan.

I put in the morning at Open Book somehow.
Mr. Hunter's jacket hung on the back of his chair like
always. You could see the lump of his keys in one pocket.
I had a handful of rocks I'd gathered down at the river
to replace them with. Gillian worked across from me all
morning. I slouched behind my book, waiting. The room
would empty at noon. I'd tell Gillian I'd catch up to her
after I went to the bank. She'd head out, Hunter would
duck down the hall to take a leak…it was a piece of cake,
and I was freaking.

Gillian looked up at me. "What's with you?"

"Nothing."

She said, "People are coming to look at our
house tonight."

"That's good, isn't it?"

She shrugged. "I guess. It's weird."

"You want to move, don't you?" I needed her to say it.

She looked at me. She bit her upper lip and tugged
her sleeves some more. She said, "My mom went on

a tidying binge last night. Now I'm supposed to cut the grass after school."

That was all it took. "You need a hand?"

She smiled. Everything in me unwound. Maybe I couldn't block her out. Maybe I didn't want to.

The lawn hadn't been cut in a long time. The front yard was all sloped, and the back was even steeper— it was terraced into four sections. You did the cutting there with an old mower that had yellow ropes attached so you could lower it down. I did the cutting, and Gillian used an electric weed whipper to trim. The air was cool, but I was sweating.

There were trees at the bottom of the yard. Beyond them was the back of another property. The house there had a patio door that opened to a weathered deck with an old gas barbecue, a glass-topped table with an umbrella and two chairs with matching cushions, all faded. The first few leaves had already turned. I worked my way down, then dragged the mower across the bottom patch of lawn. I was panting when I bent to shut off the engine. Silence rushed in. I listened to it. A bird flapped and squawked. Then I heard the scrape of a patio door opening and footsteps on planking. I looked up. Griffin was standing on his deck, looking as worn as his furniture. "It's time to talk," he said.

TWENTY-SEVEN

The silver Camry was parked a little ways up the main street. Griffin was in the front booth in Demetri's restaurant, the way he'd said he'd be. His hands were flat on the table, a mug of black coffee between them. I slung my backpack into the other seat and perched across from him, close to the aisle.

The place was almost empty; it was way past lunch and too early for dinner. A blond waitress with a cloth fanny pack full of little milk and cream containers came to take my order. I asked for a glass of water. She looked at Griffin. "Need a top-up there, Gord?"

He levered one hand up off the table like a little drawbridge. "I'm good."

We sat there, looking at each other. Maybe it sounds strange, but finally having something happen felt good, almost. Now I did my best to look worried and confused, eyebrows together, leaning forward as if I wanted to help. I'd done this a million times in the Bad Time. I could do it again. Besides, it was better to find out what he knew and what he wanted. Then I could decide how to play him.

It looked as if the waiting had gotten to Griffin too. In the brightness from the window his face was half in shadow and half lit, rutted and tired. He hadn't shaved; silver stubble gleamed on his jowls. The cuffs of his Windbreaker were grubby. His hands looked huge on the table, the fingers thick and blunt. The first two fingers on his right hand were stained yellow from his cigarettes. He didn't wear any rings. "What do you want?" I said.

"Your help," he said.

"My help? With what?"

"An investigation."

"I thought you were retired," I said. I hoped "investigation" wasn't going to turn out to be pervy cop talk for sex. He didn't look like the type, but then they never do.

"I've got one case still open," Griffin said.

The waitress brought my water. I waited for her to leave before I talked. "Why do you want me to help you? Why should I? I don't think you even like me."

"You did your reading?"

"I looked at the stupid book. I get it. You don't think I'm Danny." I shook my head as if I couldn't believe it.

Griffin said, "I don't know who you are, and I don't care."

"You know who I am," I said. I pitched my voice high. "I'm Danny." *It's not what you say, it's how you say it. Never change your story.*

"No you're not. I lived with him in my head for months. You're not him."

If this was the best he could do, I was laughing. I looked around, made a face. "Well, sorry I don't match your dreams. My family knows me. I don't know what else I can tell you."

"You've told me more than enough already." Griffin cocked an eyebrow. "You're good," he said, "really good, but you push it, you know? It was the bit about your eyes tipped me. I knew it, but I double-checked anyway. You can't change eye color. If you're interested, here's some info on it." He reached down to the seat beside him and tossed a file folder onto the table.

I ignored it. "Then how come mine got changed?" I said.

"Because you're a liar. And you're not Danny."

"I wasn't lying. I told you what they did to me. Maybe they know a little more than you do. Maybe things have—have *changed* since you retired. And they did stuff to my hands too, remember? Just like *you* said." I waved my hands, doing exasperation.

Griffin nodded. We could have been chewing the fat about the weather. "You liked that, didn't you? I could see you go for it, and you didn't push it quite as hard—it was a good play. Except if they'd altered your prints, you would have had sore feet. You didn't say anything about that."

Now I *was* confused. "What?"

"The only known case of surgically altered prints came from down your way, bud. Tucson, Arizona. A doctor grafted skin from a guy's heels onto his fingers. The poor bastard could barely walk after."

I swore to myself and took a drink of water to stall. I could feel sweat starting to run under my T-shirt. "Then I don't know. Maybe they just tried. They had me all drugged up. It doesn't matter, does it? You said yourself there aren't any prints to check."

"Maybe I lied. Maybe I'll just take that glass after you're finished and have it checked."

I slid it across the table to him. It was all I could do. "Take it right now, for all I care."

The big hands didn't move. "If I do, it won't be for the prints. I didn't lie about those. Kids' prints don't last." The eyebrow cocked again. "But there'll be a nice DNA sample there on the rim. That should be easy enough to check against someone in the family."

I shut down my move to grab back the glass. It was only a twitch, but he saw it—I know he did. "See? You're good," Griffin said, "and you're also a heartless little prick."

"All I can tell you is what they did to me." *Never change your story.*

He blinked once, a lazy snake. "And all I can tell you is what you've done and what's going to happen to you. Leaving aside how you've abused Shannon and her family's trust and emotions, you're up to your neck in it.

Fraud, perjury on your statement, probable larceny and possession of false documents. Oh, and manslaughter. Murder, if they can prove intent."

"*What?*"

"There was a guy chasing you in that Tucson parking lot. You and your traveling buddy Davidson had key-gamed him, remember?"

Fat Boy. I flashed on him, purple-faced and panting. I shook my head as if I was mystified. Griffin said, "He had a heart attack. He died a couple of days later. Tucson coppers didn't follow up because of all the sympathy for you, acting under duress and all. When I show them you're a fake, they're going to love the chance to get you back, especially if you can't prove you're a minor."

The sweat was pouring now. I could feel my face burning. He had to be bluffing. "I don't believe you," I said. It sounded strangled.

Griffin shrugged and went on. "And then there's the big picture. You've crossed the border under false pretenses. These days, they're going to think terrorism. I'm guessing everybody's going to want you—FBI, Homeland Security, our RCMP…"

My feet started bouncing under the table. I couldn't cave. I wouldn't cave, ever, to guys like Griffin. I shook my head slowly, getting my breathing under control. "Why are you doing this to me?"

"Because somebody did something to Danny Dellomondo."

"To me! Somebody did something to me!"

He still didn't move. "To Danny."

"Then look at this." I went for angry. "Who else is gonna have this?" I yanked open my backpack and fumbled through the socks I'd tossed in. The broken neck chain with the letter *D* was in them. I don't know why I thought of it. I didn't even really think it would do much good, except I knew I had to change the pace, throw him off. I tossed it on the table. "Who else is gonna have this, huh?"

Griffin looked at it, then his eyes darted back up to me. No more lazy snake. But no little cloud of confusion either. I cursed inside. "Where'd you get it?" he said.

"I've always had it. It's mine. The fastener got broken a long time ago."

"All these years?"

"All these years. Like a lucky charm. It was all I had left."

"You didn't have it in Tucson."

"Who says?"

"They inventoried everything you had."

"So?" I shrugged. "It was under my insole. They didn't look."

"Who gave it to you?"

"It was a birthday present."

"It was a Christmas present."

"How do you know?" I gave him the Danny sneer.

"That's what the family told me. Danny was wearing it when he disappeared."

For the first time in weeks, I flashed on what I'd memorized back in Josh's office. *Blue puffy vest…purple and black backpack…gold chain with the letter* D *around my neck…*and for a half beat I thought I had him. "So, what more do you *want?*"

"I want Danny and you're not him." He did the blink again. "Which means, whoever gave this to you knows what happened to him. *Comprendez?*"

That's when I stopped breathing.

"Now stop shitting me," Griffin said. "You're not an idiot. You know this is murder, and it always has been. You've walked right into the middle of it."

He didn't move. I couldn't.

TWENTY-EIGHT

All I could do was stick with it. *Never change your story.* "Well, sorry to disappoint you, but I'm alive and I'm here."

"Give it up," Griffin said. "We're past this. Danny's dead. He's been dead for three years."

"Oh, that's why I've been away. I forgot."

"He never went away. Ty killed him and said Danny hadn't come home, to cover his ass. When Ty's really flying, he's a violent guy. He'd beaten on all of them before. That's why Danny was in foster care—or had you forgotten that part?

"Riiiight," I said. "So why didn't you nail him, great detective?"

"Not enough evidence. There was no body, for one. And when the family found out he was a suspect, they backed his story."

"That's crazy. Why wouldn't they turn him in?"

"You don't know much about families, do you? Maybe they'd rather lose one than two."

A bead of moisture slid down the water glass. I swallowed. I had to ask, but I kept it sarcastic-sounding. "And so they're all in on it, this big plot?"

Griffin shook his head. "Not the extended family. The mother knows. Carleen knows for sure."

"What about Shannon?" I kept my hands flat on the table, like his, but my knees were revving.

"What do you think?"

That one threw me; it was so close to home. The best I could do was, "Well, she *better* think I'm her brother."

"I'm not sure which would be worse," Griffin said, "knowing the lie or finding out later. If you had a conscience, that question would be keeping you up nights."

"Does it keep you up nights? Or do you just want to send her to jail too?"

"She's already in jail with that family. I wish she wasn't."

There was one last question I needed to ask. I had a sick feeling I already knew the answer. "So if I'm a fake, and they know it, why aren't they turning me in?"

"If you don't know, you're not as smart as I thought. You're the ultimate alibi. Ty can't be a killer if Danny's back home. Why do you think he gave you that chain? To seal the deal, in case you know more than you're

letting on. You've got them the way I've got you, and
they know it."

For an instant I thought I saw daylight. "Well, if
they sealed the deal"—I gave him the Danny smirk—
"I guess you're screwed, aren't you? You haven't got
anybody. If they say I'm real…"

Griffin's thumb rubbed at his nicotine stains. "You're
still not listening. You asked what I wanted, I told you.
Now, we can deal on this or…" He shifted his bulk
forward and pulled out a cell phone. He punched something in, put it flat on the table and turned the screen
to me. There were three phone numbers. "The first one,"
Griffin said, "is for a guy I know in the States, used to
be with the FBI in Buffalo; now he's with Homeland
Security. The second is a friend in our RCMP. The
third is a copper I talked to in Tucson. I told you
before, but I guess you didn't get it. You blew it with
the eyes. One call from me about someone crossing the
border under a false identity and possibly setting up
a sleeper cell in southern Ontario, and they'll be on you
like a ton of bricks, no matter what the family says." He
gave me a long look. "Especially with that black hair
and those cheekbones. I mean, they're not *supposed* to
profile…What's your real family's background?"

I was too stunned to even make a face.

"Just asking," Griffin said. "Anyway, from there,
well, the DNA test will be the only part that doesn't hurt.

You know about waterboarding? Just between you and me, they still do it, but you won't die unless you have a weak heart. Your Tucson problem might be worse, if it's murder. I hope you can prove you're a juvenile. Otherwise, they have the death penalty there, don't they?"

I started to shake. I snatched my hands off the table. "This is *crazy,*" I said. "You're crazy. You won't believe me, no matter what."

"Eyes don't lie," said Griffin. I wanted to jam my fingers in his. "Time to deal, no?" I didn't say anything. I couldn't give in. Griffin spun the phone back around. "Last chance." I was shaking so hard, I thought I'd fly apart. "Let's see..." Griffin's thumb hovered over the touch pad. "Maybe start with Jimmy at the Mounties. Then he can make the other calls. More official that way."

His thumb started down. "Wait," I blurted.

His thumb stopped. Griffin looked up from under his eyebrows. I went with the only thing I had left. "Look. You won't believe me, okay. That's your hang-up. If you're gonna persecute me like this, I give up. I'll just go. I'll clear out, run off again. That what you want?" I tried to zip my backpack. I couldn't make my fingers work. I clutched the fabric instead. "That what you want? It'll rip Shan apart again too, but what do you care about that?"

The last part got him. Maybe. At least, he squinted out the window for a moment before answering. He huffed a breath out his nose, then looked back at me with those cement eyes. "You're not going anywhere now. I gave you a chance to run, and you didn't. Now I'm running you."

"Then what do you really *want?*"

"I told you. You're going to help me with an investigation."

TWENTY-NINE

I got back to Shan's just before supper. I wasn't hungry.
The microwave was humming. The TV was blaring
in the living room. She was on the phone. She put her
hand over it. "I thought you were going to be late."

"Didn't take as long as I thought."

She turned back to the phone and said something
about turkey. I dumped my backpack, watching her.
I needed to be alone and I couldn't stand to be. Did
she know or didn't she? I needed a sign from her. Shan
clicked off the phone. "Gram and Grampy won't be here
for Thanksgiving. They'll have already left for Florida."
She sounded a little pissed. Then she sighed. "I better get
a turkey tomorrow while the sale's on."

"Thanksgiving?" I said, just to say something. "We're
not even near Halloween yet."

She gave me a look and walked to the fridge. "You wanna try that again, hon?"

"Huh?"

"Thanksgiving comes before Halloween—unless you've turned American." Her voice was sharp. Was she still pissed from the phone call—or was she was pissed at my mistake? She yanked open the fridge, took out a bottle of ranch dressing and a bag of baby carrots and put them on the counter, not looking at me. She started dumping carrots into a bowl. I couldn't read her. I didn't know what the hell she was talking about, but I knew I had to play along. "What…? But…riiight! Oh, God…" I shook my head and slumped into one of the kitchen chairs. "Sorry. It wasn't like Thanksgiving was a big day for me the last three years, you know?"

"Aw, hon…it's okay. Sorry, I know. I forgot. I was just…never mind. Anyway, Gram and Grampy will be down to visit before they head south, and if you get confused about stuff like that, don't be embarrassed to just check the calendar." She waved to where it hung, above the phone cradle. "Any time."

I nodded. It sounded as if I was off the hook. "Anyway," she was saying, "Thanksgiving first, then Halloween. Welcome back to Canada. Got it?"

"Halloween?" said Brooklynne, bouncing into the kitchen. "When?"

"Not for a long time yet," Shan said, stooping to scoop her up. "Then comes Danny's birthday."

"Danny's birthday? When?"

"November tenth," I said, probably too fast. "I'll be sixteen. But Halloween first. What do you want to be?"

"Ooooooh yes," said Shan, jiggling Brooklynne. "Who do you want to be? Pretending to be somebody is so much fun, isn't it?"

"I want to be Ariel," said Brooklynne. "I'm hungry."

"Well, grab some of those carrots, missy." Shan leaned her toward the bowl and Brooklynne grabbed some. Shan started into the living room with her. "Supper won't be long. Soon as Daddy's home."

She looked at me as she stepped through the doorway. Did she jerk her head at the calendar or was Brooklynne just tugging at her? I stepped over to the counter. Canadian Thanksgiving was on Columbus Day, October 12. American Thanksgiving was November 26. Danny's birthday was Monday, November 9.

THIRTY

Harley once told me the scariest thing that had ever happened to him was when he and Darla were doing Bill and Bonnie Blessing. "It was a one-stop," Harley had said, "in and out. Soul's Light Missionary Church in Milwaukee, way up there in the boonies. I'll never forget it."

He and I were playing a round at a mini-putt course in Wichita, waiting for a guy with a cooler full of counterfeit twenties, when he told me about it. It was boiling hot and they had umbrellas up at the start of each hole. I could feel the sun grilling the back of my neck every time I bent over my ball. We were playing for Cokes. Harley always had to play for something. He putted past a Tweety Bird with spinning legs, then went on talking as he waited for me. "It was a bad vibe, you know? The pastor was this no-neck ten-by-ten who'd played defensive tackle or something for the Packers. Got *Christian Soldier* with a barbed wire halo tattooed on his arm. Biceps the size of your head." He popped a gum bubble as I putted. "Sorry. Whoo, baby. How'd you end up over *there*?"

We walked down to the balls. "You want gum?" he asked as I lined up my shot. I shook my head, then missed. He sank his putt. We walked to the next umbrella. Harley went on with the story. There was no rush; we were the only people on the course, except for a maintenance guy pretending to rake gravel. "So, I start the usual little tussle with him about what the split's gonna be on the take from the service. Usually you lie to each other about expenses, pretend to pray on it, then cut the deal. I'm away here."

"Away" was a golf word Harley liked to use, as if he was a real golfer. It meant he got to go first. He rapped his ball off the side of a miniature windmill, missing the tunnel. He swore. *Yess,* I thought. I put my ball down on the rubber mat. "Be careful," Harley said. "It's trickier than it looks."

I believed him and missed the tunnel. "See?" he said, before going on. "But that day I was way over the top, burned out. We'd been busy on the road a solid month. I'd been doing pills and a little blow to keep up, vodka to smooth things down. Bad combo, but those services were tough. Took a lot out of you, all that whoop-de-do—you remember. Anyway, Darla had warned me it was showing, and sure enough, the guy's giving me the hairy eyeball, not budging on the percentages. He *knows*, you know, and if God tells him to, he can snap me like a matchstick. And I know he knows, so in the middle of this, I just snap myself. I think, *Screw it, we're outta here*, and I'm flying so high I'm about to tell Mister Defensive End where he can stick his church"—Harley putted through the windmill—"when there's a knock on the door. Secretary tells him Mrs. Hummel's here for the laying on of hands."

He stopped for my shot. I putted through the windmill. My ball stopped maybe an inch before the hole.

"Nice," Harley said. He moved his own ball away from the backstop, closer to the hole. "Just so's I can swing the club—or do you want to call this hole a draw?"

"Putt," I said. He missed. I tapped in. He missed again before he holed the putt. I made sure to watch him mark the score. We walked to the next umbrella. "I can't remember who's away," he said.

"I am," I said. "But what happened?" I didn't want to leave the shade yet.

"Right. So as Man Mountain Wisconsin starts to get up, I hear myself say, 'Brother, let me.' To this day I have zero idea what I thought I was going to do— strangle Mrs. Hummel, whoever she was, cop a feel, piss on the desk. I don't know. But I zip out of the room and *bammo*, Mrs. Hummel is right in front of me, in a wheelchair. She makes the Green Bay Packer look like a little kid.

She's three-fifty if she's an ounce. Cans like watermelons sagging to her knees. Her husband is the seventh dwarf in a feed cap, can barely push the chair. They tell me she's got some kind of blockage, growth, I don't know, in her throat and that the doctors say she has to have an operation. She can't eat anymore.

"I'm still flying, so I say, 'Maybe that's a blessing in disguise, but I am for sure, so let us pray for fatter times instead of lean. Get your cap off there, Sneezy.' Then I muscle in behind the chair and grab her neck. It's like a bag of warm chicken fat—my fingers just sink on in. Like to gag me out right there, you know? But I bow my head and spread my legs to brace myself, as if it's third and one on the forty with a minute left to play, and I bellow out, 'O LORD...' and I open my mouth for the usual, but what's running through my head is this nonsense speed rap, *block that kick Green Bay Crapper before I wring this damn neck, Lord,* and all the time I'm squeezing the chicken fat and what comes out is, 'Unpack the block in the neck dam, Lord, in this green pray.' Then I let go and raise my hands and do my standard 'His blessings on you through me'—you remember.

"And that's when I got scared. I looked over at the Green Bay Crapper, and from the look on his face, I figured he was going to tear me apart—except he wasn't looking at me. He was staring at Big Mama in the wheelchair. And that's when I got really scared, because when

I looked, she was turning purple and shaking, and she started to cough and then she spewed out this green-black slop. Stank like a skunk in a burning tire. Then she's gasping, 'I can…I can…I'm saved…'

"I've never been so freaked in my life. It was so perfect, I flashed for a second that they'd set me up, but they hadn't." Harley shook his head at the memory of it, staring off past the battered Wonderland castle that was the eighteenth hole. "Those cheeseheads flipped out, crying, 'Praise the Lord,' hugging me, and all I could do was stare at my hands. I hadn't even felt anything."

"So it was like a miracle?" I said.

"I dunno what the hell it was. There are no miracles. I mean, if there's a God, he's gonna deal you your crappy life and answer my bullshit fake prayer? You better hope there's not a God like that."

"But something good came out of it." I put my ball on the mat. This hole had a drawbridge opening and closing.

"Anything good ever come outta your life? I'll tell you what good came out of it," Harley said, then: "You sure you got that lined up right?" I tried to ignore him. I was pissed with him talking about my life. "The good was, the Green Bay Crapper puts his arm around my shoulders and whispers, 'Fifty-fifty.' But you know what? I said, 'Forget it, we gotta go.' Darla was pissed. She said we could have raked it in after that, and she was right too. But I was so spooked I couldn't do it."

"Why?"

"Because I didn't know what was going on," said Harley. "Everything was out of control." I putted. The drawbridge opened. My ball went in the water. "Let me show you how it's done," Harley said.

I hadn't known what he was talking about then. Now I did. In the middle of the night I got up and peered out the bedroom window, between the frame and the shade. A silver Camry was parked outside. Inside it, a red speck flared once and faded. It felt like a searchlight, pointed at me.

THIRTY-ONE

The deal was, if I could find out where Danny's body was, Griffin would let me run. Pumping Ty was my Get Out of Jail Free card.

I met Griffin the next night in the lot across the park from the library. I'd told Shan I was going to the library and then to Gillian's. The Camry was parked in the shadow of a maple that was starting to turn color. I got in the back. "Keep your hood up and your head down till I tell you," Griffin said. He started the car.

I don't know what route he drove. I hunched low and watched light and shadow glide across the upholstery. It stank of dead cigarettes, like the couch at one of my foster homes. The vibration of the car synced with the fear humming in my gut. There were no streetlights now, just darkness, and the car kept rolling. "I think I might be sick back here," I told him.

"We'll be there soon," was all I got back. The car slowed. I felt it bump off the road. A little farther, then we stopped. "Wait," Griffin said. He got out of the car. I waited. A moment later he opened my door. "Out and inside."

We were out of town, parked behind some kind of barn or shed. A chilly breeze rustled the weeds—maybe we were close to the lake. The fresh air felt good. Griffin swung the barn door, and we went inside.

The place was dim and full of smells and junk: lumber, fence wire, tires, windows, an old Volkswagen. The dirt on the floor looked oily. Griffin pulled a string and light leaked from a bare bulb in the rafters. "Where are we?"

"It doesn't matter." He led me behind a pile of boards. He had a plastic grocery bag. He took out white surgical tape and the box that held a battery-pack transmitter and the wire. "Pull up your shirt." The chill grabbed at me. Griffin put on latex gloves. He was fast and efficient. He taped the transmitter to the small of my back. "Drop your pants." He ran the wire under my crotch and up the center of my chest. The tape nagged at me every time I moved, glowing even whiter than my skin in the shadows.

"What do I say?"

He shrugged and tore off another piece of tape from the roll. "You're the crap expert."

"What if I don't get him?"

"First, you may not get him tonight—it might take a little time. Second, I got nothing to do for the rest of my life. I'll come after you even if you run, and so will Homeland, the Mounties, FBI, you name it. You'll be looking over your shoulder until one of us gets you. And I guarantee you'll wish it's me. Lift your chin higher."

"What if I can't?"

"Don't kid me. Bullshit is right up your alley." He adjusted the wire and pressed the tape to my chest.

"What if you're wrong?"

"Sometimes I wish I was. But I'm not. Okay, we're done." I pulled my jeans up and my shirt down. Griffin reached back into the plastic bag and handed me what looked like a joint in plastic wrap. "Put it in your pocket. Give it to him. It'll mellow him out and put you in good. He'll start talking anyway."

We left the barn and drove again, me hunched in the back. I did what he told me. I couldn't see any other way. When he finally let me sit up, I had to slouch to keep the transmitter from digging into my back. Griffin lit a cigarette and cracked his window. A rush of road noise and cool air found me. "I'm not going to ask who you are," he said over it.

And there it was again, my favorite question. "Danny,"
I said. I knew it was pathetic now, and I knew I could
have told him anything, but I wasn't giving up my last
shred of...whatever—dignity, I guess. And in some weird
way, I couldn't let Shan down. Griffin didn't say anything,
just held his cigarette by the open window. The slipstream
blew the smoke right back in to me. I said, "Why are you
doing this?"

"I'm old-fashioned. I believe in truth and justice."

"Shan already hates you." I wanted to rub something
in. "You'll flip her out."

"It's not a nice thought to face, is it? One of your
brothers murdering the other. I guess that means she's
going to hate you too—if she doesn't already."

I wasn't going to think about that. I pushed harder.
"Doesn't that bother you?"

"Sure, it bothers me. Does it bother you how you've
abused that family's trust?"

"What have I done except make them happy?"

Griffin took a last drag and flicked the half-smoked butt
out the window. "You can't live a lie," he said. "It's a cancer."

"You are so wrong," I muttered.

"What was that?"

"Nothing."

"Happiness isn't truth." Griffin put up his window.

This time he was right. Happiness was *better*.

It was maybe half an hour to Peterborough. It was
deep twilight now. We drove to a neighborhood of

dumpy old houses. Griffin showed me Ty's place as we
rolled past. It was especially crappy, with a mattress on
the patch of front lawn and some two-by-fours propping
up one end of the porch roof. He parked the car just
around the corner and opened the glove compartment.
The receiver for the wire was the size of an electric shaver.
He plugged it into the dashboard outlet and unspooled
an earbud connection. Then he looked at me in the rear-
view mirror. "Ground floor, back, number two. Front
door's always open. He'll be there—he always is, this
time of night. When you turn the corner out here, say
something as a test. I'll flash my lights if it's working.
If I don't, come back here." I looked away and nodded,
shrinking deeper into my hoodie. Griffin popped in the
earpiece. "Got the joint?" I nodded again. "It'll get you
in the door, get him started if nothing else. Then take
your time, see what you can get. Like I said before, we
may have to do this more than once."

The hell with that, I thought. It was now or never.
I swung the car door open.

"And…" Griffin said. I turned. "Be careful. He's
jumpy as hell, even when he's stoned. We don't need
anything happening to you"—I started to get out—
"before this is done." I slammed the door.

THIRTY-TWO

I had the shakes again. I stuffed my hands into the pouch of the hoodie and thought about running, but I knew it wouldn't help. I walked to the corner. The sidewalk was wet; the grass glistened under the street and house lights. It must have rained earlier—I hadn't noticed. "Test," I mumbled. "Danny counts one, two, three." I glanced back. The Camry's lights flashed.

Up close, Ty's place looked even worse. The rain-soaked mattress on the lawn had scorch marks on it and wads of burnt stuffing exploding from one end. The yard was all empties. One of the porch steps was broken, and the storm door hung wide open. It had no glass, just a torn screen. I pulled my hand into my sleeve before I tried the main door—I didn't want anything connecting me with this place.

The door was unlocked, like Griffin had said it would be. Inside was a cramped hallway. The scuff marks on the walls were lit by a tilting ceiling fixture. There were stairs on the right, battered little mailboxes on the left. Beside the mailboxes was a door with a black number one on a slanted gold sticker. At the end of the hall was a two. Between them, a kitchen space and a bathroom, doors open, were competing with the reek of weed to see which could smell worst. There was no sound.

I thought again about running. Then I shut the front door softly and cat-footed down the cracked lino to Ty's door. Now I could hear shuffling sounds and the dribble of hip-hop from earbuds. I kept my hand in my sleeve and tapped. The door felt about as sturdy as cardboard. "Ty?" I kept my head down, trying to muffle my voice. Nothing. I tapped harder. The door wobbled under my knuckles. The tinny hip-hop got louder, as if a bud had popped loose. The shuffling got closer.

"What, what?" from behind the door.

"It's me," I said, keeping my voice low.

"What, who?"

I had to go for it. "It's *me*, Danny," I hissed.

The door jerked open a few inches. Ty looked out at me, more like death than ever. I could tell he didn't recognize me. "Hey," I said. He focused on me; his eyes flared and he sucked in his breath. Then he did that neck-roll thing and said, "Ah, ah, not now, dude. Not a good time." He started to close the door.

I actually shoved my foot forward, like some cheesy salesman. "C'mon, Ty, we gotta talk," I said, patting my pocket.

His eyes flicked down. More twitching. "You holding, dude?"

I nodded. He stepped back and I slipped in, close enough to smell whatever the hell was on his breath.

The room had a table, a chair, a floor lamp and a mattress with a sleeping bag crumpled on it. 50 Cent glared down from one wall. On the opposite wall there was a fist-sized hole in the plaster. A Confederate flag draped the window. There was a pile of clothes in one corner and a bong beside the mattress. The floor was a litter of empties, sub wrappers, cardboard slice triangles, what I guessed were crack pipes, and a couple of mini gas bottles like the ones Harley used to have for a portable barbecue. It was cold in there, but I was sweating. I could feel the surgical tape, the transmitter, the wire, all clutching at me. I wondered if it picked up my heart racing. "Whattaya got?" Ty said. He was twitching up a storm. His earbuds were dangling, still rasping away.

I fished out the joint and tossed it to him. He missed the catch, then pounced on it, hands and knees, as it landed beside what might have been the top of a little blowtorch. "That's it?"

"Whaddaya want? Those suckers cost, dude. It's for you. To say thanks, like." Already I was mimicking him. I wasn't even trying.

"No worries, no worries." He had it out of the wrap and was snapping a lighter, still kneeling in the crap on the floor. He wore a grubby camo hoodie. The pocket on the right side bulged. The bulge was the size of a lot of things, all of them bad. I took a step back and bumped the table. A plastic soda bottle rolled to the floor. Ty didn't notice—he was too busy sucking on the joint. I hooked the chair closer with my foot. I figured I could hit him with it if I had to.

Ty let out a long jet of smoke and flopped onto the mattress, back against the wall. His eyes were still bouncing everywhere, but they kept coming back to me. "So…little bro…" Now his feet were jerking around too.

"How you hangin'?" I said.

"Dude, you don't wanna hear. Don't wanna know."

"Sure I do."

"Well, I'm not so good, man. Cupboard's bare. Not feeling…up to snuff, you know?" He gave an electric little cackle, then took another toke and waved the joint. "I was thinking some bad thoughts, just now, before you come."

"What kind of bad thoughts?" I wished I was closer to the door, just in case.

"Don't wanna know, dude, don't wanna. Bad, bad thoughts, things comin' back…But brother W helps, dude. Helps…"

"Good," I said. "I just wanted to pass on a little thank-you, 'kay?"

His eyes got narrow and shrewd. Stoner shrewd. Harley had always told me that heavy dopers get paranoid. "What for?"

I took a breath, felt my way. "Well, I've been…hearing things, you know?"

He went rigid. "What kind of things, dude?"

"Just really weird shit, man. About you—and that people thought…"

He erupted into jerks and neck twisting. His hand wobbled over the big pocket, then he hit on the joint again, like his life depended on it. As he blew out he said, "Who's…saying stuff?"

Now I was going an inch at a time. I couldn't take my eyes off him. "Well…like, the cops? They were all over me, you know…and they…"

"IT'S NOT TRUE!" I was ready for it, but I still flinched, jolting the table. Ty slapped the pocket, snarling. Ash from the joint spilled onto his leg and the mattress. There wasn't much more than a roach left now.

It was too scary. I started easing toward the door. I forced a deep breath, held up my hands, did my best casual. "Well, duh. 'Course it's not true. I'm here, aren't I?"

He jerked and settled back down, except for one foot that kept kicking. Only now something was different: the other foot was digging into the mattress, and he was pressing himself back against the wall, almost as if he was trying to get away from me. He did the neck twist and took a stab at a smile. "That's right. Absolutely, dude, absolutely. You're back." Ty's right hand with the roach was on the bulging pocket. His mouth was open and his wired eyes were locked on mine, but the look wasn't stoner shrewd anymore. At first I didn't know what it was. Then I did: he was scared. That was all I needed.

Back in the Bad Time, sometimes I'd take it out on even littler kids at schools. All it took was that same look in their eyes, and I'd be on them. I could feel myself changing gears, taking control. Griffin was right— I had words, now that the time had come. It felt so good, I never stopped to think they might be the wrong ones. "That's why I appreciate you giving me the chain, man." I held my hands palms up, as if this was a no-brainer. I heard my voice get confidential. "That sucker is, like, worth its weight in gold to me. It was in my description."

"No shit? No worries, dude."

"So, like you said, we're in it together? All the way?"

"What? Yeah, yeah, all the way." He was pushing away so hard I thought he'd go through the wall. I tried not to look at the hand.

"*Ex*cellent. So, listen, I wanted to give you something back to show it's the real deal, that I'll keep it together, you know?"

"Sure, sure. Okay. I'm all for that, dude."

I put one hand on the chair and leaned forward. "Sweet." I was almost purring. "So where did you put him?"

"Wha—?"

"Where'd you put him? Where's the body?"

He scrabbled back from me like some kind of giant insect. His head started snapping around like it would fly right off his neck. He hissed, "What are you—don't even *say* that, man!"

"No, listen. Don't you see? You tell me what you did with his body, it makes me an accessory. I can never tell or I go down too. You've got my secret, I've got yours. We're bound together, like blood brothers or whatever."

His eyes glittered crazily. "I don't…I don't know what—"

"Sure you do," I coaxed. "I got to tell you, weird as it sounds, I was glad when I figured out what you'd done for me with the chain. I mean, all at once I knew I wasn't alone in it anymore. I knew that you had my back. It was a good feeling. I want to give that to you, man. Brothers in blood, back to back."

"Get *outta* here."

"Come on, Ty. You're feeling sick with it. Share the load; you'll feel better."

"You think *I'm* sick," Ty shouted. "*You're* sick. You're a maniac. You're…you're…"

"I'm what? Pretending to be a dead kid to his family?"

"HE'S NOT DEAD!"

"No, I'm not. I'm not dead, am I? Danny's not dead, is he?" I waved my hand around the room. "*This* is dead. Tell me, and you won't be."

"Yes, we will." Ty kept twisting back, as if he was hearing a sound behind his shoulder. "We *are* dead. We're dead, dude. Dead, dead, dead. That's why we're here. And we both know it. I thought about it a whole, whole lot, all the time. Only diff is, you're here forever and I'm not."

Before I could move, his hand jumped into the pocket. As I grabbed the chair, he jerked something out and stuck it in his mouth. I saw what it was as he pulled the trigger. I never heard the shot. I'm pretty sure I screamed at the same time, but I never heard that either. His head snapped back and something blotched the wall behind him and I was gone.

THIRTY-THREE

I ran blind, I don't know how far, before I realized the Camry was rolling beside me. Griffin pulled ahead and up to the curb. The passenger door opened. "Get in." I was past thinking. I got in.

He drove fast but carefully, not saying anything. I was hunched up, knees to elbows, hyperventilating, trying not to see red blossoming behind Ty's head, puddling behind Harley's. I heard Griffin say, "Where'd he shoot?"

"His mou—" I gagged, and he pulled over. We were on the two-lane highway. I staggered through a muddy ditch, the puke already spilling from my mouth, and heaved and heaved in the long grass by a fence. I scrabbled under my clothes and ripped off the tape and wire and threw them as far as I could. When I turned around, panting and acid-mouthed, I was almost surprised to see the car was still there. I got back in and we pulled away. "I didn't know he had a gun," Griffin said. He didn't look at me.

We took some kind of backroad into Port Hope. As we started down it, Griffin said, "What's done is done. Maybe it's better this way. In that place, they may not find him for days. There's no connect. You'll be long gone."

I looked at him. He was clutching the wheel with both hands, looking straight ahead. He said, "The guy in Tucson didn't die." He looked a thousand years old, and I hated him for every second of them. I said, "You got nothing on me now anyway. You try telling anyone, and I'll tell them about this. I'll tell them how you assaulted me sticking on that wire." I spat on the dash. I spat on the seat. I clawed the roof liner and armrests, then started swiping at everything around me. "And they'll find my fucking DNA all over your car no matter how much you clean it—and all over you." Then I lost it and started swiping at him, hitting him. He had his arm up to keep me off and the car was swerving and then he backhanded me across the face. It hurt like hell. I yelled and stopped hitting. I couldn't breathe right. I touched my face. Blood was running from my nose. More blood. It was all over my hand. My face was throbbing, but everything inside me had gone flat and cold. I moved my hand around, flicking it to spatter my blood all around the interior. Then I slowly rubbed a big smear into that gray upholstery. "That'll cost you your max from the bank machine," I said. "Unless you're just going to kill me." I was so far gone right then, I don't think I would have cared if he had.

He got me the money. I stood by his car while he did. Nobody was around. In Port Hope, they rolled up the sidewalks at six o'clock. "Go," he said. I knew I would, but I wasn't telling him that. I shouldered my backpack. "Maybe I'll see you around," I said. I took a step away, then turned back to him. "Sure hope you were right about Ty."

I meant it as a last shot at him, to get under his skin forever, but as soon as I said it, I thought I was going to be sick again. Griffin didn't say anything. He got in the Camry and started it up.

THIRTY-FOUR

I walked. I knew I had to go, but then I'd always known that. I even had money in my pocket. Blood money, I guess. I should have been planning, but I was in a fog. The pain in my face was fading, but my nose and cheek felt puffy and tender. I didn't even know where I was going until I realized I was walking up the hill to Gillian's. When I saw where I was, I stopped and stood there for a long minute. I knew I had things to do before I left.

Knowing that was a strange feeling, like a dog tugging the wrong way on a leash. I'd never had it before. I was trying to decide how to get to Gillian without her mom knowing and asking questions when the front door of her house opened. Gillian came out into the porch light, frowning, with Buster on his leash, and started down the driveway. That was when I noticed the SOLD sticker on the real-estate sign.

She saw me as Buster dragged her forward to say hi. Her face got even cloudier when she got a better look at me. "What happened to you?"

"Aw, I was skateboarding with Matt and I messed up." All at once I felt nervous. "Your house sold."

She didn't answer. She was pulling tissues out of her pocket. She handed them to me. I wiped around my nose. It hurt. "Why are you out so late?" I asked, trying to put things off.

"What do you mean? It's only eight thirty."

"Oh! Right. Wow, maybe I hit a little harder than I thought. Anyway, I was coming to see you."

She took a tissue from me and dabbed at my face. It might have been the first time I ever wanted someone to keep touching me. She said, flat-voiced, "We're moving."

"When?"

"Soon. A month." She looked away.

For an instant I wondered if I could hang on a month. Ty's brain exploded behind my eyes again. I said, "Is that good or bad?"

She looked back at me. "I don't know." She paused. "Right now it feels bad."

"Where are you going?" It was so weird. It couldn't make any difference now, but knowing she was going felt like another part of me was getting torn away.

"Montreal," she said. "It's cheaper, and that's where my mom's family is."

I touched her hand, then my cheek. "Can you just wipe here, like? It feels good." She raised her hand again. I guided it on my face. "Maybe it will be better than here."

"Why should it be?"

I didn't know. I said, "Well…"

She said quietly, "You won't be there." She lowered her hand, and then I was kind of reaching out mine and we were holding on to each other, not quite hugging. I could feel the dog straining at his leash. "We better walk," I said.

We started down the hill, still holding hands. I knew the easy thing to do would be to just say "See you tomorrow" and be long gone by morning. Maybe it would even be the best thing, I told myself, because when the questions started flying, Gillian wouldn't know anything. I'd be protecting her. But I wanted to give her something so that later she'd know she was special, that I hadn't just blown her off like one more Bad Time family I'd worked over. I remembered the birthday card. "Listen," I said, "I've got something for you." I let go of her hand and found the card in its envelope in the top pocket of my backpack. "Here." I handed it to her. "We— I mean, you—won't be here in February."

She opened the envelope as we walked. "You bought it!" She looked at me, brighter. "You could have mailed it."

"It wouldn't be the same. And I wouldn't know the address."

"I'd give it to you, silly." She opened the card. "But you didn't sign it."

"Aw…" I said.

"You have to sign it. Come on, over here." By now we were at the bottom of her street, in the park across from the library. She led me over to a picnic table and put the card down. Buster stopped to do his business. Gillian followed him with a plastic bag from her pocket.

I got my pen out of my pack and bent over the card, but when Gillian came back I still hadn't signed. "You don't have to say anything fancy," she said.

I was staring at the blank space. I felt paralyzed. Finally I said, "I can't sign." My voice was wobbly.

"Why not?"

I forced it out. "I don't know my name."

Gillian touched my back. "What do you mean? Are you okay?"

It was now or never. "I'm not Danny."

She sat beside me. She smiled. "You keep saying that."

"I know, but I'm *not* Danny and I never was. The real Danny disappeared three years ago and never came back. I saw his name somewhere and pretended to be him to get out of some trouble I was in."

Her face blanked. She pulled back. "Then who are you?"

The Question. I swallowed. "I don't know."

"What do you mean, you don't know?"

I looked away. The ache in my face got hotter. Buster sniffed around the table. I said, "I don't know anything. I don't know who my parents were. I was given up when I was born. They called me a ward of the state and I got put in all these foster homes from when I was a baby. That was the Bad Time. I don't know my real name. I don't even know if I have one. Someone picked one. Sometimes people would call me by one they liked better. I don't even know my birthday for sure. I knew it once, but nothing ever happened on my birthday and then I started lying about it and got confused. Harley—this guy I was with—he got paid to take me from some people who said I ran away. I was with him for a long time. Then he had an accident and died and I was scared I'd go back, and I heard about Danny and I lied, just to get away. I had to—I was scared of the Bad Time. I never thought it would turn into this." I closed my eyes. "I'm nobody. I've done bad stuff. And now I have to go too. I was coming to say goodbye. I can't do this anymore, and it's bad to you. You can't…live a lie." The last words hurt the worst. I didn't dare look at her.

Gillian was quiet for what seemed like a long time, and then she said, "I can tell you who you are. You're somebody who is smart, and nice to me when nobody else wants to be. You're the person who makes Shannon and Matt and Brooklynne happy. You take chances. You're brave. You do things on your own. You don't care what other people think."

"I lie," I said. "I fake, I cheat, I steal. I…" The sick was bubbling up in me again. "I make…I make people do bad things. Harley had his accident because of me, and once…I made a guy kill himself."

"Oh, come on," Gillian said.

"The first time you saw me I was stealing, to show off to Matt. You were right. Then I lied to you after."

I looked at her then. Her face had fallen. Her hands were in her jacket sleeves. She pushed up her glasses and got to her feet, tugging at Buster's leash. "Come on," she said to the dog.

I'd said too much. It was like a can of soda exploding— I couldn't stop once I'd started, and now I'd ruined everything. Maybe that was what I deserved, but I didn't want it to end this way. Maybe Gillian didn't either, because she didn't go anywhere. Instead, she said, "Are you lying to me now?"

"I could be, but I'm not. At school that day, I needed to talk to you so bad."

"Because of my name." I nodded. "Where did you know a Gillian?"

A month ago, I would have snowed her with a story about a little sister I'd gotten separated from or a best friend in grade one. Now I told her: "She was a girl in a book I read over and over. She kept getting moved around like me, and it never worked out for her either, except once and then she had to leave."

"*The Great Gilly Hopkins*," Gillian said flatly. "So you never knew her. That's a lie too."

"No. I *knew* her. I can't—she was just like me. It was like she was my only friend and she got out and it was like if she could, maybe I…I can't explain."

"I get it," she said, more gently. Then: "Remember what you said to me the first day at school? *Be anybody you want?* Maybe you get to be."

"What?"

"Be anybody you want. Be someone who doesn't lie and cheat and steal."

I looked at her. For once in my life, I didn't know what to say. What finally came out was, "Give me a name."

She looked off toward the library, then closed her eyes. When she opened them she said, "Adam."

"Adam?"

"It's the first name. You're starting at the beginning."

"Adam." It felt right. "Thank you," I said.

"Sign the card, Adam," she said softly.

I signed. I didn't know what my signature would look like, but it turned out okay.

I gave it to Gillian and said, "You can start at the beginning too."

"No, I can't. People in Montreal will know."

"But it's not your fault your father—"

"Maybe it is. Maybe if I wasn't so shitty…" She started to cry then. I wanted to touch her so bad. I lifted a hand and stopped.

"No," I said. "Listen, I've hung with guys like your dad. They're the jerks and losers."

Gillian hit me as I sat there. Buster yelped. On top of Griffin's backhander, it really hurt. I pushed on anyway. "And I'm no better. I'm one too. You're the good one." I grabbed my pack. "I'm sorry," I said. "I better go."

"Are you really going?" She was sobbing.

"Yes," I said. Back when I'd let myself feel, I'd felt bad in lots of ways, but never like this.

"When?"

I took a deep breath. "Tonight. That cop, Griffin. He's out to get me."

"Tonight? So this is…where will you go?"

"Just…away," I said. "Work a traveling carnival." I didn't tell her it was the wrong season. "Maybe it'll come to Montreal." And then we were just holding each other, my face buried in her jacket. "Anyway," I said into her shoulder, "I can't stay here if you're going to be gone."

She held me tighter. I heard her say, "I'll go with you."

It stopped me dead. For an instant, the whole world opened up. Then it shut down. "You can't. You have to stick with your sister and your mom."

"But what about Shan?"

"If I stay, I'll bring her more trouble than ever."

Gillian let me go. Her glasses were crooked and her face was tear-stained. I looked at her and for the first time since I was little, I thought I was going to cry.

She straightened her glasses. "Be Adam," she said.

THIRTY-FIVE

Now Gillian wiped her face. "I have to go. My mom will be calling any second." I stood up. She said, "Something fell out of your pack." Buster was sniffing at whatever it was. She bent down and lifted a folded piece of paper from the grass. It was the page of Young Harley mug shots. Part of one of the photos was showing. Gillian unfolded the paper. "Who is this?"

"It's some old pictures of the guy who took me away from the Bad Time. The one who died."

"Was he a crook?"

"Kind of, I guess. Kind of a friend, too." I'd never thought of Harley that way before, but now, in a way, it felt true.

Gillian stared at the photos. "That's wild. Well, I can see why he took you." She refolded the paper and handed it back to me.

"Why? Because they paid him."

She squinted at me. "That's not what I meant. You look just like him."

"What?"

"You do. It's like an older you, with a moustache and bad hair."

I didn't know what to say. I unfolded the paper and looked at Young Harley. I had no idea what she was talking about. Young Harley gave me the same blank, smart-ass look he always did. Me? That was me? It was too much. I put the paper in my pack and walked back up the hill with Gillian. Just before we got to her place, I tugged at her sleeve. "Gillian." We stopped and kissed. It was mostly teeth. I was pretty bad at it.

"Sorry. I've never done this before," I said, and it was true.

"That's okay," Gillian said. "Neither have I."

"We could try again."

It was better the second time. Gillian's cell phone rang in her pocket. We stopped kissing. "That'll be my mom," she said. "I have to go." Up at her house, I could see the front door was open.

"I have your email," I said. "I have your cell."

She nodded. I patted Buster and she was gone.

I watched from the shadows until Gillian and her mom were inside. Then I walked; I had to keep moving. I told myself I was making a plan for how to get away as fast as I could, but I was tired and wired and my mind kept drifting. To Gillian. To Michael Bennett Davidson, 61472, out of Dayton, Ohio; arrests in San Fran and Portland, might have lived in Portland for a while. To me shouting and Harley lying in the parking lot, his head in that red puddle. To Ty. And then I'd start trembling. I told myself it was getting cold. I started for the little railway station, thinking I could just hang there until the morning train. I knew it would be deserted at night: there were only two trains a day that stopped in town. But when I got there, a police cruiser was idling in the parking lot, and I flashed crazily that Griffin had ratted me out. I turned away. I'd known where I had to go all along.

THIRTY-SIX

I went back to the park and wrote a note, but I knew it wasn't good enough. I put it in my pocket anyway. When I got to Shan's house, Gram and Grampy's RV was parked in the driveway. The house was dark except for the glow from the stove light in the kitchen. I knew she'd be in there. I knew it wasn't the first time and probably wouldn't be the last that Shan would be sitting up alone in the kitchen, waiting for someone to come home. Sure enough, when I went around and slipped through the kitchen door, she was sitting at the table in her pink fluffy housecoat, the cordless phone and her World's Best Mom mug in front of her. I stayed in the doorway.

"Gram and Grampy are here?"

"They're asleep in the RV."

I nodded. Shan said, "You're not coming in, are you?" Her lip trembled.

"Something bad happened," I said. "I have to go."

She looked down. "Don't tell me anything. I don't want to know."

"I—"

"No," she said. "Don't. Please." She gripped her mug with both hands.

"Shan—"

"NO!" She slammed the mug down on the table. It shattered. What was left of her tea splashed out, and a line of red began to trickle across one of her thumbs. I tore some paper towels from the holder under the kitchen cupboard. She wrapped them around her thumb and put her hands in her lap. She was crying now, but silently, her eyes screwed shut and her shoulders shaking.

I sat down at the table, across from her. "Will you tell me something? You don't have to."

She didn't answer for a long time. Then she said, "What?"

I knew what I wanted to ask, but I didn't know how to ask it. "Did…Do you…"

Shan looked up at me. Her cheeks were streaked with wet. "I just wanted everything to be *right*."

It was all I was going to get. Maybe I didn't need any more. I reached over and pushed at the pieces of broken mug in their tea puddle.

"You really are…" I said.

"Wh-what?"

"That." I pushed the shard of mug toward her that said *World's Best*. "Thank you," I said. "I wish I could stay."

"Then why don't you?" It was her last shot.

It took me a long time to find an answer. Finally I said, "I'm a different person now."

Shan closed her eyes. Outside, a car rolled by. Across the kitchen, the tap dripped. Time leaking down the drain. She nodded.

I stood up. "I won't take anything," I said.

She looked at me. "Where—no, I don't want to know. How?"

I shrugged. "I'll just go."

"That's—" She shook her head, pulling herself back together. "No, there's a way." Now she looked right at me, a look as sharp as the shards of mug on the table. I nodded. I'd had the same idea. "All right," she said. "Leave a note."

"I don't know what to—"

"For Christ's sake," she snapped. "Leave a note. Tell the kids you'll miss them. Tell—leave *me* a note." She stood up and moved to the counter, scrounged up a pen and paper and pushed them at me. This time I wrote:

Dear Shan and everybody

Im sorry but I have to go. I have tried hard but Ive been so long away that I cant fit here anymore. Maybe it doesn't help but I told you a lie about what happened to me. I didnt get taken. I ran. It was bad with Ty and Momma before and

I couldn't take it any more. I didn't want to say that when I came back. Some bad things happened to me while I was away but nothing I couldnt handle. Being away is what I am used to now. Please don't come after me it is better this way. Im sorry if I hurt you.

    love

    Danny

When I was done, I folded it up and gave it to Shan. She didn't try to read it. "Now," she said. "Go up and get some sleep. I'll call you."

THIRTY-SEVEN

The next morning, Gram and Grampy stopped for coffee and a washroom break right across the border, in Watertown, New York. When I guessed they'd be well away from the RV, I let myself out of the little closet near the back that I'd crammed into as they'd had breakfast in Shan's kitchen. I needed to go pretty bad myself. It was a bright fall day as I slipped away. I had my pack with some clothes, Griffin's money, Harley's mug shots and a couple books. Danny's neck chain I'd slipped into Shan's purse, on top of her car keys. Gillian's email address and cell number were in my head.

I'm not going to tell you where I am now. I'm not going to tell you how much time has gone by. Let's just say I'm all right and I'm in the territories.

If you ever read *Huckleberry Finn*, you'll know what I mean. Maybe you've even been there.

Sometimes it's been scary and sometimes okay. I've served your burgers and poured your coffee and loaded your shopping cart. I've shared a squat with you. I've sold you clothes and books. I've lined up with you at food banks and shelters and bus stops and libraries and clinics. I've sat beside you in freshman English, said yes to you in improv class, even been in a TV commercial you saw and two plays you didn't. I've taken your drinks order and recommended a wine. I've done a lot of things, including some I'm not proud of. I've never forgotten.

I might be called Adam Davidson, Ben Adams, David Adamson, Adam Gillian, Gill Adams. Or Sean Callahan. Or Frank Rolfe. The name doesn't really matter, does it? I'm short. I'm a pretty fast runner. I don't like marshmallows. I keep to myself. I try not to take dumb chances, just do what I have to do. I think I'm loyal. I think I know what's true. I know where I've been. I know where I want to go. Montreal is on that list. One day I'm going to Portland, Oregon, to check the birth records for March 29, 19—well, never mind the year. In the meantime, I send birthday emails to Shan and Gillian. I miss them.

Maybe you'll meet me. Maybe we've already met. It doesn't matter. I could be anybody, but I'll know who I am.

AUTHOR'S NOTE

This is a work of fiction. The characters and incidents I describe are purely imaginary. However, the situation at the heart of my story—an imposter claiming to be a missing child—does come from real life. I stumbled upon it in an article by the American journalist David Grann, "The Chameleon," which appeared in the August 11 & 18, 2008, issue of *The New Yorker*. In it, Grann told the almost unbelievable story of a Frenchman in his twenties who, in 1997, impersonated a missing teen from San Antonio, Texas. Anyone looking for proof that truth is stranger than fiction need look no further than Grann's reporting. (The story became the subject of a British documentary film, *The Imposter*, released in 2012, which at the time of this writing I have not seen.)

Grann's reporting led me to wonder about a character who's not just an adept imposter, but someone who literally doesn't know who he is—a kind of permanent imposter. My story took its own path from there.

ACKNOWLEDGMENTS

As I mention in my author's note, the spark for this novel came from David Grann's superb non-fiction piece in *The New Yorker*. Without that to fire my imagination, there'd be no *Who I'm Not*. My thanks to him.

I also owe a big debt to many people closer to home for their support, encouragement and willingness to be pestered while I was writing a book that was more than a small change of pace for me. My longtime friend and colleague Peter Carver stands in the front rank.

My thanks as well to David Bennett at the Transatlantic Agency for his enthusiasm and energy on behalf of the book, and for two key insights that became crucial to shaping my story.

I'd also like to acknowledge the assistance of the Ontario Arts Council via a Writers' Reserve Grant, and thank Richard Dionne of Red Deer Press for helping make that possible. It was greatly appreciated.

My friend and neighbor Mark Vandervennen, executive director of the Shalem Mental Health Network, helped me understand how "Danny" would experience the world. His vast experience with kids like my main character kept things in focus. I'm grateful.

And, of course, my thanks to everyone at Orca, particularly Andrew for his quick support of this project and to the ever-patient, ever-logical Sarah "Why? What's *that* about?" Harvey, who so deftly edits my ramblings.

Finally, as always, the biggest thanks go to my son Will and my better half, Margaret. I'd only light out for the territories if they came too.

TED STAUNTON is a writer, speaker, workshop leader, storyteller and musical performer. His novel *Jump Cut* was part of Seven (the series) and he is the author of many other books, including the Morgan series for young readers, the picture book, *Puddleman,* and two titles in the Orca Currents series. He lives in Port Hope, Ontario. To learn more about Ted, visit his website at www.tedstauntonbooks.com.